Meet the commander and crew of the Valiant.
The elite intelligence force known as . . .

SPACE HAWKS

COMMANDER BRYAN KELLY. The Admiral's son whose early mission ended in disaster. *Valiant* is his chance to redeem himself . . .

DR. ANTOINETTE BEAULIEU. The brilliant but disillusioned ship's medic, she's already been forced out of the service once. She has a lot to prove.

CAESAR SAMMS. The only surviving member of Kelly's first command, he's tough, loyal, and battle-hardened—but his carefree lack of caution can ruin them all . . .

PHILA MOHATSA. The volatile junior operative whose secret past on a frontier planet has trained her in the use of exotic—and illegal—killing tools . . .

OLAF SIGGERSON. An older, more experienced civilian pilot, pressed into service, who rarely agrees with Commander Kelly's judgment.

OPERATIVE 41. The genetically altered half Salukan, dependable, but cold and impartial—who can be sure where his true alliance lies?

FULL SPEED AHEAD—
ADVENTURE AWAITS!

Ace Books by Sean Dalton

SPACE HAWKS
SPACE HAWKS 2: CODE NAME PEREGRINE

BOOK TWO

CODE NAME PEREGRINE

Sean Dalton

This book is an Ace original edition,
and has never been previously published.

CODE NAME PEREGRINE

An Ace Book / published by arrangement with
the author

PRINTING HISTORY
Ace edition / September 1990

Cover art by Wayne Barlowe.

For information address: The Berkley Publishing Group,
200 Madison Avenue, New York, NY 10016.

ISBN: 0-441-11362-1

Ace Books are published by The Berkley Publishing Group,
200 Madison Avenue, New York, New York 10016.

PRINTED IN THE UNITED STATES OF AMERICA

10 9 8 7 6 5 4 3 2 1

CODE NAME PEREGRINE

1

O glorious city, tender haven of coolness . . . thy light shines as a jewel in Pharaon's crown.

—from the *History of Byiul*

Intense heat burned through Bryan Kelly. A dry, relentless, inescapable heat that baked his skin, dehydrating it rapidly. He couldn't breathe because the air was too hot. He blinked hard, trying to keep his eyes moist, but they were drying out. Smoke boiled through the bridge section. Around him came the screams of his crew mingled with explosions throughout the flag ship as they took another torpedo to their starboard flank. He shouted his orders over and over, but no one seemed to hear him in the chaos. To his left, the helmsman's face had been burned black. Tears streaked her face as she held course, backing them out of the battle line with salvo after salvo of enemy fire exploding around them, sapping the last of their shield reserves.

"Kelly."

Coolness broke the heat surrounding him. Kelly groaned, hearing the stern voice of the military judge calling him to rise for the verdict. He strained to hear the sentence, but the screams of the dying crew of the *Nonpareil* drowned out the judge.

A hand shook him. "Kelly! Wake up."

He blinked awake with a start. Standing over him was Caesar Samms, looking squat and awkward in his bulky white environmental suit.

"You okay, boss? You were dreaming a bad one."

"Yeah."

Kelly's mouth felt dry and puckered. His body slumped limply while he tried to pull free of the nightmare. It was the old recurrent dream of the court-martial. He hated it.

He sat up, struggling against the constrictions of his environmental suit, and pressed his hands against his face plate. Caesar stepped aside, and the sun he'd been blocking blazed down full upon Kelly once again.

Instantly he felt as though he were being baked alive. He touched a control on his belt, seeking to boost the cool temperature. A soft beep in his headset warned him that he was close to straining his power unit. Sweat trickled between his eyes. He blinked and pulled his arm from its wide sleeve to reach up inside his suit and wipe his face.

Around him stretched the featureless expanse of the Valu Desert. Flat ground, crusted white with alkali, supported no plant life. In a deep azure sky, the sun, which had dropped a fraction since Kelly fell asleep, blazed a merciless yellow-white that seared through the strong polarization of his face plate and made his skin feel as though it had dried to his cheekbones.

He clambered slowly to his feet, getting a boosting hand from Caesar, and turned around. As far as he could see in three directions, there was nothing, not a ridge, not a rock outcropping, not even a dead animal carcass lying bleached in the sun. It was disorienting, even mesmerizing. He turned southwest and stared a moment at the city of Byiul shimmering behind heat waves. It was only nine kilometers away; it looked deceptively closer. A tall mountain range stood behind the city, black and jagged against the sky.

Kelly sighed and glanced at his squad of Space Hawks, waiting with their equipment for the next move.

His mind still felt groggy with sleep. He gave himself a shake and checked his chron. Two hours had passed.

"I feel like an ant in a skillet," muttered Caesar, his voice coming tinnily over Kelly's headset.

"The heat will get worse," said Kelly, remembering his briefing.

"Yeah, it's already 158 degrees—"

"—and climbing," broke in Beaulieu.

Kelly nodded, the statistic making him feel even hotter. The Valu Desert was considered a natural defense northeast of the capital. Incapable of supporting life, it was rarely patrolled by Salukan security forces.

They didn't need to. A broad sensor grid lay across the region. Movement beyond a range of fifty-six meters in any direction crossed a sensor line, triggering an alarm. Kelly grimaced as sweat ran into his eyes. No one said getting in would be easy.

For the countless time he wished they could have teleported directly into the city, but Byiul lay under the protection of an anti-teleportation screen. The Salukans guarded their capital well.

Kelly glanced at Phila Mohatsa, who was operating the scanner. "About fourteen more minutes, Phila," he said. "Then look sharp for that grid shift."

Her yawn came over his headset. "Right, Commander," she said sleepily. "I'll be ready to mark the position change."

"I think Siggie was right," said Caesar. "We should have just blasted their satellite that controls all this fancy security gridwork."

"Siggerson *always* wants to blast satellites," retorted Phila with scorn. "He must have caught it from you."

"Keep on task," said Kelly sharply, and they shut up.

Beaulieu threw open a cooler and tossed drink packets at everyone. "Dehydration alert," she said. "And, Caesar, *don't* ask what this is."

Caesar caught both his and Kelly's, then handed one of them to Kelly with a grin. "Green packets," he said with a mock groan. "It's bound to taste worse than whatever was in the pink packets we had last time. Why can't you docs concoct a good-tasting mineral and salt supplement?"

Beaulieu ignored him and corrected 41, who still didn't

quite have the hang of feeding his packet through a sleeve airlock. 41 growled something that Kelly couldn't make out and abruptly flipped open his face plate to drink the packet contents.

"Dammit, 41!" said Beaulieu angrily. "You can't replace necessary fluids if you keep losing your environment."

41 closed his face plate without a word and tossed his emptied packet into the cooler. Kelly exchanged a look with Caesar, who rolled his eyes. Smiling, Kelly pulled his right arm free of his sleeve and unsealed the tiny airlock from inside. Pulling his packet through, he one-handedly detabbed it and lifted it to his mouth.

The first sip tasted unbelievably cool and refreshing. The second sip hit his taste buds. He choked, nearly gagged, and gulped down the rest with a shudder for the sour aftertaste.

"As soon as we get to Byiul," said Caesar, making horrible noises over the headset, "I'm going to find a Salukan bar."

"They won't let you in," said Beaulieu with a laugh.

"Pipe down," said Phila sharply. "Communications scan going over."

"Hell," said Kelly in alarm. He gestured, and they all threw themselves flat on the ground with their headsets cut off.

The silence was absolute. The hard ground radiated heat that could be felt through the suit's insulation. A layer of dust coated Kelly's face plate. He lay motionless with his shoulder against Caesar's leg and tried to breathe slowly and silently, tried to calm the thumping of his heart. He wanted desperately to see his chron, but he dared not move his arm.

Phila had switched off her scanner, and if she missed the next grid shift reference, they might as well kiss this mission and their lives goodbye.

Communications scans were rare and random, lasting anywhere from fifteen to eighty-five seconds. Phila allowed maximum time for insurance. To Kelly, lying there counting off seconds in his head, it felt like an eternity. He couldn't see her, and he didn't dare shift his head. The scan was incredibly sensitive to the slightest noise.

Finally Caesar's leg nudged him. Kelly cautiously raised himself up and saw Phila's wave of all-clear. He drew a deep breath of relief and flipped on his headset.

". . . can the chatter," Phila was saying sharply as everyone started to speak at once. "Less than one minute to grid shift."

"All right," said Kelly, standing up. "Everyone, gather equipment and prepare to move fast."

Behind him Beaulieu, Caesar, and 41 switched on the two grav-flats that rose slowly off the ground. They tossed duffles, coolers, and two scanner tripods onto the flats where weapons cases, an extremely precious Harvsk TR90 signal jammer, rope coils, hand scanners, spare environmental suits, and oxygen tanks were already strapped on. Kelly took out his binocs and sighted his bearings, taking care to reference Byiul so that they stayed on course toward the section of the city he wanted to enter.

They had just five hours before their suit batteries expired. The margin for making the city within that time range was a slim one. Nor could they wait until darkness fell, for Byiul activated a perimeter forcefield to suspend arrivals and departures. The ancient practice of locking the city up for the night also happened to be a very effective one. Kelly grimaced to himself, trying to hold down his impatience to get moving.

41 came up to stand beside Kelly in silence. He was the only one carrying a Salukan long-range rifle slung over his shoulder. All the other weapons were still in the cases.

41 was so tall the environmental suit almost didn't fit, and his face was hidden behind the polarization of his face plate. As he gazed across the desert his stance indicated restlessness. In the five months Kelly had known the ex-mercenary, he had learned that patience was not one of 41's virtues. And while 41 was always quiet, since they had teleported down to Gamael—origin world of the Salukan Empire—he had barely spoken at all.

Kelly watched him now, wary of 41's unpredictability. Alliance records had turned up nothing on the man except a couple of arrests for illegal weapons dealing and an expired slave registry from a nasty little colony moon called Harsis IV. No tax payments, no citizenship affiliations, no insurance, no birth records, no bank accounts. 41 himself remained reticent concerning his origins, and that frankly worried the head of Special Operations.

"I don't want him on this mission, Kelly," Commodore West had said gruffly in their final meeting in his office on Station 4. "It's too sensitive, and he doesn't check out. Even that drug interrogation failed. He went wild. Broke the ribs of a technician before they got him restrained. He's obviously conditioned. Hell, he's half Salukan. Sending him to Gamael with you is like equipping you with a traitor."

"I trust him," Kelly had argued. "At least against the Salukans. He won't betray us to them. And I need him."

Now they stood side by side in the alkali dust. 41 pulled out a pair of binocs and stared due east through them.

"What is it?" asked Kelly in alarm, aware of 41's superior vision. "Do you see something?"

"No," said 41. He lowered the binocs and shifted the strap of his weapon higher on his shoulder. "They will have other checks we don't know about. We are bound to trigger something."

"So far our information on this defense system has been accurate," said Kelly.

41 looked at him. "You trust too much."

Kelly had to laugh. "Perhaps I do. It's better than being paranoid."

"Paranoids live longer."

"But optimists live best."

They stared at each other a moment, then 41 made a grudging gesture of surrender. "You're getting better at the game."

"Thank you," said Kelly, pleased. He was never quite sure when 41 was joking, feeling truly pessimistic, or just being difficult. "What do you think of Gamael so far? Does anything feel familiar? Does the Valu stir your blood?"

41 turned away from him and stared east again. "I like the open space," he said at last.

"Yeah?" broke in Caesar. "I don't. If we can see them,

can't they see us? Standing out here in broad daylight makes me feel as naked as a stripper in church."

Kelly grinned and 41 said, "What is—"

"Commander," said Phila's voice. "Stand by. Relaying now."

Kelly stiffened. "Receiving."

As the bearings came over, Kelly turned his body in accordance, marking the new direction with his binocs. The desert shimmered a faint blue through them, and as he programmed in the necessary numbers, they glowed a faint red down the edges of his vision finder. 41 and Caesar pushed the grav-flats past him.

"Move!" said Kelly sharply.

He ran ahead to take the lead. The grid shift could be anywhere from two meters to sixty, in any direction. The hard part was guessing where inside the grid square they should park. If they settled too close to a sensor line, it could cross them during the shift and sound the alarm. If they settled too far in the center, they might not be able to match the grid's movement.

"Coming up on a line!" warned Phila's voice in his ears. "It's moving opposite to us. We have to cross."

"Caesar!" said Kelly.

Caesar threw himself halfway across the leading grav-flat and activated the jammer. Static filled Kelly's headset. He winced at the noise and gestured frantically for his people to hurry. They ran clumsily in the bulky suits, their feet kicking up dust clouds that hung in the air.

Let there be no visual sightings taken today, Kelly prayed.

"We're on the other side," said Phila over the static.

Caesar cut the jammer without being told. Kelly heaved out a sigh and could not help glancing back, although the sensor lines were invisible to his eyes. Panting because the smallest exertion was hellish in this heat, he took a fresh sighting and started jogging again, determined to get them as far as possible before the grid stopped shifting.

"Is it still moving?" he asked, his voice ragged.

"Yeah," gasped Phila, jogging in the rear with the scanner in her hands. "This is a long shift. We're moving at a diagonal so we might make another square. Do you want to risk jamming the line again?''

It was a gamble. Security monitors might become suspicious of faulty blackouts in the sensor lines, especially if a movement pattern was noted. On the other hand, when the sensor lines were stationary, they could not be jammed at all. Kelly hesitated only a second.

''Yes, let's go for it,'' he said. ''Keep up the pace, people.''

They seemed to run for an eternity. Kelly felt as though he were drowning in his own perspiration. His heart whumped against his ribs, and no breath was deep enough. The others struggled with him. He could hear their panting and grunts. Beaulieu, who was the oldest, worried him and he kept an eye on her when she rested her left hand upon the second grav-flat and used it to pull her along.

''Coming on another line!'' warned Phila.

Caesar switched on the jammer and they staggered on, their stumbling feet kicking up white dust that fogged about them. And Byiul shimmered out there ahead of them, looking like a mirage. Puffing hard, Kelly looked at his chron. They hadn't been at this more than fifteen minutes.

''It's stopping,'' said Phila.

''Park,'' said Kelly.

He halted and the others clustered about him, leaning upon the bobbing grav-flats or kneeling. No one seemed to have the strength to speak. But they'd covered distance. Kelly wiped his face and looked at them in approval.

''Where are we positioned in this square?'' he asked Phila when he thought she'd recovered enough to answer.

''Just inside the line,'' she said.

Kelly nodded, taking another sighting of the city. This time when he switched to maximum vision, he could see individual dwellings and movement. He fought off the urge to crouch out of sight. At this range his squad in their white suits was largely invisible to the naked eye.

Beaulieu suppled them with more drink packets, and as soon as they finished choking the unpleasant liquid down, Kelly gave the order for them to walk on.

"From now on we crowd that line," he said. "We have over two hours until the next grid shift. When it moves, I want us squatting right next to it, ready to go."

Caesar said, "We've got about four or five hours of daylight left. It's going to be close, boss. Yusus, won't we look stupid squatting outside town all night?"

"We'll be frozen stiff," said Kelly, not wanting to think about it. He saw 41 staring east again through the binocs. Frowning, Kelly said sharply, "41, are you sure you don't see anything?"

"Nothing."

Phila stood beside 41 and stared at the baking desert behind them. "Then why do you keep looking?"

41 stowed his binocs. "According to the map, there is a military installation eighty kilometers east of Byiul. If we cause suspicion, investigation will come from there."

As a theory, it made a lot of sense. Kelly nodded, satisfied that 41 was doing his job well. "Everyone, keep sharp," he said. "Just because we feel alone out here doesn't mean we are. Gamael doesn't have the reputation of being impenetrable for nothing. Now, let's move out."

Four hours and ten minutes later, 41's lean silhouette stood against the blazing sunset of scarlet, gold, and indigo. The temperature had already dropped sixty degrees, and the rest of the squad was busy shucking out of their environmental suits while 41 stood watch with the binocs. A light, refreshing breeze stirred from the south, bringing cooler air off the mountains. It fluttered the knee-length hem of 41's bright blue *chunta*, which he wore over white linen trousers, and stirred his mane of blond hair, which fell to his shoulders.

Down in the bottom of a cement-lined drainage ditch bordering the slum outskirts of Byiul, Kelly bent over to finish stepping out of his suit and inadvertently bumped into Phila. She mumbled an apology and edged away, crouching to swiftly fold her suit into a compact bundle for stowing.

Because of her diminutive size, she had been disguised as a young boy. Salukan children went shaven except for a long hairlock braided with the colors of their family and house, and Phila's bald skull gleamed faintly in the gathering dusk. Kelly had not realized just how attractive her long curly black hair was until she reported for duty with a shaven head and a fierce look that warded off any jokes or sympathy. Even now, he still felt slight shock at the sight of her. And Caesar, thank God, had not teased her once.

But Caesar's disguise . . .

Kelly glanced at him and frowned. No amount of skin tinting and hair dye had been able to turn Caesar's freckles and red thatch into anything resembling a Salukan. He was also too short and stocky. Finally the Infiltration Lab had dyed him blue, stitched fake yellow tattoos on his cheeks, and given him a Yllrian passport. He still looked Irish, but it was the best anyone could do. Besides, with luck, he wouldn't be seen by many of the natives.

Kelly finished bundling up his environmental suit and pulled on his Salukan clothes. He wore linen trousers and a *chunta* of scarlet beneath a thin yellow cloak. Shaking a headdress free of his duffle, he put it on his head, only to grimace at the fit and toss it to 41. The other headdress in the bottom of the duffle was crumpled and creased. Kelly slapped it against his leg and put it on, letting the long ends hang down his back.

"Finished?" asked Beaulieu.

She had Caesar's and Phila's suits under her arm and reached out to take Kelly's. Being black, female, and middle-aged, she could not be dyed or passed off as a boy. Surgical tucks had slanted her eyes and pointed her ears. She wore a wig of straight white hair that was surprisingly becoming.

Kelly wiped the perspiration from his face. He still half expected the bronze tint injected into his skin and his elaborate face paint to melt off, but so far it had proven impervious to moisture. He helped Beaulieu pack away the suits for later use.

Caesar squatted nearby, frowning at one of the slim, lightweight oxygen tanks and tapping the digital gauge with his finger.

"Problems?" asked Kelly. He glanced at his chron, then at the sky. They were inside the perimeter, but he wanted to take no chances at this point. It was too easy now to relax and feel like they were home free when in reality the mission was just beginning.

"No," said Caesar. "Just checking."

Phila hustled past with a fat, waterproof canister which she dropped next to Caesar. She was still breathing hard from their last run out of the desert, and perspiration glistened on her face.

Kelly tapped Caesar's shoulder. "Hurry and get the rest of your gear. We're too exposed here—"

A shout from 41 sent Kelly whipping around in time to see a single-seater aircraft skimming in low right at them. It had the setting sun behind it, making it almost invisible to the naked eye.

With an oath, Kelly shoved past Caesar and dove for the nearest weapons case.

"They must have picked up our jamming pattern and decided they needed a visual," said Caesar, digging out a Kloper charge, which he tossed to Phila. She was busy screwing together a launcher, but Kelly knew there wasn't time.

The craft was already on them, making only a faint whistling sound as its sleek body split the air.

Damn, damn, damn, Kelly thought, struggling to pop out the muzzle and stock of a Salukan rifle. He should have passed out weapons first thing when they reached the perimeter, but his orders were to make a totally unobserved entry.

No chance of that now, but setting off fireworks would only make the situation worse.

"Everybody down!" he yelled, going flat on his stomach as the craft skimmed right over the drainage ditch.

Even as he threw himself down, he rolled onto his back, struggling to get his sights on the underbody where cams were no doubt transmitting visuals back to the base. Kelly, his team, and their specialized equipment were all marked. Their only hope was that in these shadows infrared pics would be too grainy or indistinct for accurate identification as Alliance personnel.

"Ready to launch Kloper, sir!" shouted Phila breathlessly.

"The range is too close," said Caesar. "You'll take us out

in the backlash. Wait until he swings back toward the desert."

"No firing without my order," said Kelly. He was already planning their scramble as soon as the observer departed. They could still melt into the city, crowded with people here to celebrate the Pharaon's birthday. Byiul security would have a hard time spotting them.

On the bank, however, 41 knelt with his rifle in his arms and began firing at the tail from nearly point-blank range.

Kelly jumped to his feet. "No! Cease fire! Cease—"

The aircraft nosed up sharply and banked around for another pass. Kelly glared at 41 and gestured for him to get down inside the ditch. 41 ignored him and aimed his weapon again as the craft swooped for a second dive.

Fuming, Kelly started toward 41. He heard an emphatic click from the undercarriage. A chill prickled on the back of Kelly's neck. He turned and saw the perforated muzzles now lowered from the belly of the aircraft. Shouting, he brought up his own weapon just as 41 started firing again.

The vicious *sphut-sphut-sphut* of strafing filled the air, and chips of cement ricocheted.

"Out of the ditch!" yelled Kelly.

Caesar, Beaulieu, and Phila scrambled up the steep sides. Kelly held his ground, trying as 41 was trying to hit the right spot on that sleek, impervious hull. But there was no stopping it as it whistled closer with flame shooting from its belly, and there wasn't time for the squad to completely clear the ditch.

The blast of hot air swirling beneath the craft hit Kelly in the face. A tracery of bullets headed right for him. Pinned there with the cement wall against his shoulder, he fired steadily until his weapon thrummed in his arms. At the last moment, he threw his rifle on top of the bank and jumped for it, clinging halfway up with chips of cement and bullets whizzing around him. One nicked his heel with a jolt that numbed his foot. He lost his fingerhold and slid back down into the ditch, scraping his cheek on the rough cement.

41 was still firing from the bank, using his limited supply of armored mini-missiles with throaty coughs from the lower

muzzle of his rifle. Kelly caught his breath and hobbled toward the launcher and its Kloper charge lying where Phila had abandoned it. He snatched it up, throwing the carbonite stock over his shoulder and flipping up the sights. Furiously blinking sweat from his eyes, Kelly didn't care if the observer crashed in the middle of those nearby houses; it was going down.

He saw the observer shift slightly to the right, obviously aiming at 41. Dirt and bullets flew, and Caesar shouted something. Kelly sighted quickly. But the warning light still blinked in his sights, and he didn't dare risk the consequences of the deadly backlash at this close range.

Damning the pilot under his breath, he forced himself to hold fire. Launching the Kloper prematurely wouldn't save 41 now. And yet . . . Kelly didn't want to sacrifice an operative just for a good shot. He didn't want to be this cold, this patient. He . . .

The tail of the aircraft blossomed orange. A split second later Kelly heard the dull boom of the explosion, a sound that rapidly crescendoed into a deafening roar. Heat and the force of the concussion knocked Kelly back, sending him skidding on the ground.

A queer wail came from the craft and it veered sharply toward the desert, plowing into the ground with a larger explosion that rocked the world momentarily. Kelly huddled in the bottom of the ditch with the unfired launcher in his arms, cringing from the rain of dirt and debris falling from the air.

The following silence seemed endless. Slowly Kelly pulled himself upright and walked unsteadily to the side of the ditch. In the distance he heard faint shouting and the wail of a siren. Right now it didn't seem to matter.

"Boss?" called Caesar's voice softly. "Hey, boss, you down there in one piece?"

Kelly blinked and realized he was resting his cheek against the cool wall. This was no time for indulging in reactions. He shook off his grogginess.

"Yeah," he said. "Pull me out."

Caesar gave him a helping hand. Kelly glanced at him and Phila.

"Everyone all right?"

They nodded. In relief Kelly clapped them both on the shoulder. "Where's Beaulieu?"

Caesar jerked his thumb over his shoulder. "Headed to find the pieces of 41. Who got it? You or him?"

"He did," said Kelly grimly, handing over the launcher.

"Poor devil." Caesar folded the launcher with three brisk snaps. "If he hadn't been so alert, we'd have been caught with our pants down."

Kelly nodded, feeling rage swell up in his throat. It never changed, whether he'd worked with an operative for a short time or for years. Raw, angry grief burned the back of his throat.

As soon as he regained control of his voice, he said, "We haven't much time. You and Phila get down there and round up your gear. Go on with your job. Don't wait for us."

"Right." Caesar nodded in the flickering light cast by the fire from the crash. "The citizens are already crawling out to have a little look."

Kelly looked and saw a few figures in the distance. He swore softly to himself and ran along the bank, crouching low to make himself less visible against the backdrop of flames.

"Beaulieu!" he said urgently. "Come on. We haven't—"

She was kneeling a short distance ahead of him and glanced over her shoulder. "Give me a hand. He's unconscious."

Kelly nearly stumbled in his surprise. He dropped beside Beaulieu and put his hand on 41's arm. In the near darkness, all he could see of 41 was a sprawled shadow. "He's still alive?"

"Got a good pulse," she said crisply. "The extent of his injuries can't be determined here without—"

"Later," said Kelly, capping off his surge of relief. "We have to clear out now."

Sirens wailed closer. When Kelly jumped back down into the ditch, Beaulieu helped lower 41 to him. Kelly got 41's slack body over his shoulder, grunting a little under 41's weight. Beaulieu scrambled down unaided and hurried ahead of him to collect the gear Caesar and Phila had left behind on the remaining grav-flat. By the time Kelly got there, she had it moving along the ditch. Kelly lowered 41 onto it, and the flat bobbed low beneath his additional weight. 41 made no sound. Worried, Kelly curled his fingers around the operative's wrist and felt his pulse. Still strong and steady.

He got behind the flat and pushed it along fast, letting Beaulieu lead the way.

According to their map, the ditch curved around and entered a cheap residential quarter, where it then tied into the sewer system. The plan had been to follow the ditch as far as it could take them, then merge into the city population as just another trio of inhabitants.

Now it looked like there would be no chance of that, for Kelly heard the distinctive chopping sound of another search-and-surveillance craft approaching overhead. A blinding spotlight snapped on, stabbing through the darkness and playing over the burning wreckage.

Kelly involuntarily ducked, although the searchlight wasn't aimed in this direction . . . yet. He quickened his pace, hearing the soft slaps of Beaulieu's running feet ahead of him.

Their swift departure saved them, for the fire attracted the entire attention of the search crafts for several minutes. By the time the searchers swung out in a wider pattern, Kelly and Beaulieu were hurrying through the residential section. Mud walls towered over them and they followed the curve of the ditch until it petered out. The tall walls sloped down to a flat depression with a large metal drain across the bottom.

Kelly glanced swiftly around. They needed a hiding place for the grav-flat. He found it in a broken wall that had tumbled down in a couple of places. Running ahead, Kelly remembered to wrap the ends of his headdress across his face before he peered through the break in the wall.

He saw the shadowy outlines of a courtyard overgrown with weeds dried to husks. No lights shone from the house and one side of its sloping roof looked as though it had fallen. Satisfied, he turned and gestured at Beaulieu to shove the grav-flat over.

When she joined him, still breathing hard from their run, Kelly scanned the sky where the two search crafts had become three. They were fanning out systematically now. There wasn't much time.

Feeling uncomfortably exposed, Kelly unloaded gear as fast as he could. 41 stirred, groaning softly. At once Beaulieu opened her medikit and produced a hand scanner. Kelly saw the soft green light reflecting against her palm as she moved it across 41.

Kelly took 41's arm and helped him sit up. "Easy. Try to stand."

41 put a hand to his head, but Kelly tugged insistently until he finally slid off the flat and stood swaying.

"He shouldn't be moving around yet," said Beaulieu.

"Get him into the courtyard out of sight," said Kelly with another anxious glance at the night sky.

She followed orders. When Kelly finished clearing the gear boxes off the flat, he tilted it on end and floated it through the break into the courtyard. Then he went after their equipment, taking care to make as little noise as possible. He could hear muffled sounds from behind neighboring walls, but so far no one had ventured out to the ditch.

Wiping sweat from his face, Kelly gathered the last duffle and weapons case under his arms and crawled into the courtyard for the last time. 41 and Beaulieu weren't in sight. He nodded in approval and started hunting a place suitable for his cache. The search would eventually go from house to house, and a deserted dwelling would be where they'd look first. However, if the Salukans used scanners set for life readings, they might not take the time to personally enter every dwelling on this street.

He had to risk it. There wasn't time to do anything else.

With some tricky maneuvering, he managed to float the flat into the house. The interior smelled musty and sour as though vermin had lived in it for a while. Snapping on his microtorch, Kelly shone the light around with his fingers cupped over the end. Trash and dirt drifted across the stone floor. A table with broken legs lay on its side in one corner; otherwise, there were no furnishings. Kelly depowered the gravflat and left it resting on the floor.

Swiftly he sorted their gear into two stacks. The fat duffle containing their environment suits which would recharge themselves, the cooler of rations, and the scanner calibrated to the Valu defense grid would stay here. To the side of the cooler, he affixed a tiny, very expensive device which created a miniature waver shield. It would last only three hours, but by then the search should be over.

"Commander?"

At the sound of Beaulieu's deep voice, Kelly turned sharply and crunched his way toward her.

"How is he?"

"Very shaky." Her hand gripped his arm in the darkness and led him into the next room. "Head wound. Serious concussion. Some lacerations. He needs to be kept quiet and under close observation for a couple of days—"

"Damn." Kelly squatted down beside 41, who sat leaning against a wall. "We've got to get out of here. The sooner we blend with the population, the—"

"I can walk," said 41, starting to get up.

Beaulieu stopped him. "What is your name?" she asked.

41 struggled against her restraining hand. "I said I can walk!"

Beaulieu didn't budge. "What is your rank?"

"Operate all four legs and the rest will follow . . ." 41's voice trailed off.

"Who am I?"

41 sat in silence a moment while Kelly watched him in growing worry. Leaning back against the wall, 41 finally said, "Doc."

"Okay. Who are you?"

"Not . . ."

Beaulieu took Kelly's torch and held up three fingers in the light. "How many fingers do you see?"

41's face looked gaunt and pale. A sheen of sweat covered his skin. His blond hair was matted with drying blood at the temple. Kelly watched him trying hard to focus on Beaulieu's hand, but his pupils didn't look right.

"Three," he said at last. "And . . . and I'm 41. Darshon, what a headache."

Beaulieu sat back on her heels and met Kelly's gaze without a word. Kelly bit his lip but he had no real choice.

"We have to move. Give him something to hold him together until he can get some rest."

Beaulieu frowned. "Commander, that's not wise—"

"Getting caught holed up in here isn't wise either," Kelly snapped, and rose to his feet. "Do it!"

Minutes later they emerged cautiously from the house and slipped through the shadows just as a searcher swooped low over nearby houses. An amplified voice called for the inhabitants to come out and line up in the street. Hitching the fifty-one-pound jammer higher on his shoulders, Kelly herded Beaulieu and 41 faster.

They cleared the quarter at last, slipping into the crowd watching a parade of dignitaries and passing tableaux of various glorious moments of the Pharaon's life. Under the streetlights, 41 was streaked with dirt and blood, his bright blue *chunta* torn, his walk unsteady, although Kelly and Beaulieu kept him pressed between them. Too noticeable. Kelly soon steered them down a poorly lit street.

Pausing to let 41 rest, Kelly paced beside their pile of gear while Beaulieu did her best to clean 41's face. With his headdress wrapped across his nose and mouth, he looked more passable. And his tawny eyes were less hazy. They met Kelly's gaze.

"I can do my part," he said, sounding tired but more coherent than before. "No changes of schedule."

Relief spread through Kelly. "You're sure?"

"Of course not," broke in Beaulieu sharply. "He's just saying that. There's no way we're going to separate—"

Kelly frowned. "We've attracted enough attention as it is. The more quietly we filter into place, the less likely we are to be picked up."

Beaulieu's dark eyes flashed angrily. "He acts better, but exertion could bring on a fainting spell or temporary loss of memory. You can't mess around with a concussion, Kelly. At least let me go with him."

Kelly thought it over and shook his head. "We'll all stick together."

"No!" said 41. He jerked down the ends of his headdress, and a line of white ringed his mouth. "I am able to work. I do not need an attendant."

Kelly gripped his arm. "We're taking the risk."

41's eyes blazed back. "You are a fool. I can do my—"

"41, stop trying to be so damned independent," said Beaulieu. She gripped his other arm. "On your feet. We've got a contact to meet."

41's gaze flickered from her to Kelly and back to her again. "As you wish, *Commander* Beaulieu."

Her face darkened. She glanced at Kelly as though to speak, but he gave her a smile and a slight shake of his head.

"Let's go," he said. "Keep a sharp watch for troopers."

They started slowly down the street. 41 frowned at Kelly. "I will not break," he said. "Do not care so hard."

"It's called teamwork," said Kelly in annoyance. "Now, try to look drunk."

2

Stealth is thy walk; fear is thy sword.
—epitaph of Rienjeth II

In the administration wing of Godinye Prison, the Mailord Cocipec paced slowly back and forth in his office, grimly watching a report on the Sang Quarter crash, which had occurred an hour earlier. So far he had permitted the military to investigate the matter. DUR—the Pharaon's secret police—did not concern itself with common insurgencies. But Cocipec had predicted the Alliance would attempt to assassinate the Pharaon during Carnival, and he believed this breach of Byiul security marked the initial phase of that attempt. He waited now for proof, for an arrest, for a sighting of an Earther, for an abandoned piece of equipment of Alliance manufacture.

The report, however, gave him nothing to support his theory. The facts themselves were few: the Valu defense grid showed a jamming pattern of its sensor lines indicating sophisticated movement across the desert; an observation Sharpskeet located five individuals within Byiul perimeters; infrared scanning recorded Salukans handling equipment not yet completely identified; the Sharpskeet exchanged fire with the insurgents; the Sharpskeet crashed, killing the pilot; no other casualties.

"Off!" said Cocipec.

The viewscreen blanked. His aide Krilit, uniformed in the soft green tunic and black trousers of DUR executive branch, watched him attentively. Idly thumping his abdomen plate, Cocipec paced yet again about his office. Rebellions happened all the time. This was yet another small attempt at insurrection, already failed. Yet his instincts said otherwise.

Cocipec frowned, wondering if he had become one of those fools who force all evidence to support a theory rather than keeping an open mind.

He paused and glared at Krilit. "Nothing has been added to this report? No other data?"

"No, Mailord."

A tone chimed discreetly on his comm. The aide hastened to answer it. He listened a moment, then put down the handset.

"It's nothing, just a reminder of the Mailord's social obligations this evening."

Cocipec snorted. A diplomatic reception at the Tamere Embassy, where lavish entertainment and food would be served in honor of the Pharaon, who would not attend. Tamere was a minor world belonging to the Empire; he could be late if he chose and the ambassador would not dare be offended.

Rubbing his right eye, Cocipec said, "The report mentioned some equipment which was not identifiable. Why not?"

"There is no specification. The recording could be faulty. Infrared often is. Or they have not yet—"

"Don't speculate on the military's behalf," said Cocipec impatiently. "I want specifications requested."

"Yes, Mailord."

"And I want a direct interview with the officer in charge of this investigation."

"Yes, Mailord."

Cocipec thought a moment, then picked up the handset and called Specialist Firult over a private, scrambled line allowing no access to military snoops. Firult answered immediately in the way a good specialist on duty should. But Firult was no gled-faced promotion seeker; he honestly reveled in his job and put it before everything.

"Is your department ready to work overtime?" asked Cocipec.

Firult's eagerness came over the line like a palpable force. "The crash in Sang Quarter? What do you want us to do?"

Cocipec hesitated. He could drop his theory and simply wait for developments. That was all his duty required of him.

But military investigators could botch evidence and blunder. Cocipec knew he was right; he had to follow his instincts.

"I want a net spread. Five Earthers may have entered Byiul. I want them found."

Firult did not immediately answer. Cocipec could imagine what he was thinking. Byiul's population numbered 18 million. With the influx of loyal subjects eager to glimpse the Pharaon during these days of Carnival, that number had swelled.

"Concentrate on the Royal Quarter and the areas bordering the Defended City," said Cocipec. "That narrows the surveillance sufficiently."

"Yes, Mailord," said Firult. "Five Earthers will stand out, even in disguise."

Cocipec laughed. "Ahe! Look for short people."

"When do we start, Mailord?"

"Immediately. Concentrate upon known dissidents. Any residents who are pro-treaty should be watched. Use as many men as necessary."

Firult drew an audible breath. "Thank you, Mailord. Then we have official sanction?"

"No."

Cocipec caught Krilit frowning and knew he was risking too much. If there were no Earthers, he would fall from office as swiftly as a gromet shot from the sky. It could not be helped.

"You must keep quiet about what you are doing. Just maintain the net and hunt for them. But do not cross the military investigators. That's an order."

"Yes, Mailord."

Cocipec cut the connection and left his office, with Krilit following three correct paces behind. He passed two security checks on his way out and paused at the exit for the sentry to lower the forcefield. Even so, Cocipec's personal bodyguard emerged first, shielding Cocipec with his own bulk until the launch purred up against the steps. Only then did the bodyguard step aside and allow Cocipec to emerge.

The evening air had cooled enough to make him glad of his light cloak. He inhaled the scent of the canal lapping at the stone steps of the complex, enjoying the moisture evaporating off the surface of the water.

Behind him, Godinye towered tall and silent. No windows opened from the external walls, giving the complex a dark, ominous atmosphere. Godinye was the state prison, where political prisoners or those who seriously displeased the Pharaon entered, often never to appear again. Unlike some of his colleagues in DUR, Cocipec did not particularly enjoy striking terror into hearts each time he entered a room. But such power had its uses.

Smiling slightly to himself, he stepped aboard his launch. "I want to stop at Rafael's," he told his aide.

"A gift for your hostess, Mailord?"

Cocipec's smile faded. Krilit was a fool. After three months in Cocipec's employ, he could not yet make obvious connections between Cocipec's personal actions and ongoing investigations. Rafael's was a gathering place for mild dissidents. Cocipec had long suspected it was a drop point for information, but his agents had never proven it.

When the launch passed beneath Tupsetshe Bridge and docked at Stolat Quay, Cocipec trotted up the stone steps to the street, with his aide and guard following. The quay was crowded with early revelers, many of them costumed and masked in historical fashion. But Cocipec in his uniform of dark green and black with the distinctive iron skull hanging at his throat had no difficulty getting through. Civilians drew hastily out of his way, and he progressed quickly down a narrow alley between two moldering old palaces here in Royal Quarter, smelling moss and dampness beneath the stench of burnt incense.

Emerging upon busy Stolat Road, where traffic blared in a rapid free-for-all, Cocipec turned right and entered Rafael's halfway down the block.

The fish shop was narrow, with a curved glass front converted into tanks of brightly colored myllets and darters. A cluster of strollers stood outside the shop as always, attracted by the display of fish. Inside, queer shivery light from myriad tanks played green and light blue tints across the faces of customers. Panels of alabaster carved into stylized aquatic motifs hung on the walls. The center of the shop displayed a rectangular pool where fleshy crimson poud-flowers bloomed and huge white kyrp swam lazily beneath the surface.

Cocipec's gaze narrowed. He never entered without feeling suspicious, although nothing appeared amiss. Customers crowded the shop, many of them young huns of the best houses, guarded and richly dressed in silk wigs and jewels. No one even vaguely resembled an Earther. Rafael did not cater to aliens, so Cocipec did not see any of the other species of the Empire here either.

Cocipec stepped past a lean boy wearing the sand-hued emblem of Genisset House and stood in a clear spot where the proprietor could see him.

Within seconds Rafael came puffing down an aisle to greet him. Cocipec responded coolly and told Rafael what he wanted. Then he watched Rafael scurry to select a small crystal globe-shaped bowl and catch a fragile blue creature of wavery long feelers and gossamer fins banded in lavender and green.

Rafael's frame was mounded with fat that bulged and quivered with every movement. He looked massive in a shapeless black *chunta*, and even in the cool of evening he constantly perspired, puffing for air like one of his fish. His skin was sleek and repellently translucent, pale and sallow enough to make him look unhealthy. Being only of a tribe, he did not shave his skull, nor did he wear a wig. His own hair was a dingy brown, touched here and there with golden highlights.

It clung damply to his temples in limp hanks. Immense popularity had made him a rich shopkeeper.

But as he came puffing now in triumph with the exotic fish fluttering inside the crystal globe, Cocipec met those limpid brown eyes and felt fresh distrust. Rafael liked to appear good-natured and stupid, but he was highly intelligent. Cocipec approved the selection, watching Rafael to see if the man looked more cheerful than usual. Or a touch worried beneath the facade.

Neither. Annoyed, Cocipec signaled for his aide to pay.

''Do you listen to city news, Rafael?'' asked Cocipec.

Rafael paused from digging in his money tray for change and bowed as deeply as his fat would permit. ''Sometimes, Mailord.''

Several heads turned their way. Cocipec knew it was rare for an officer of his rank to engage in idle chat with a middle-class shopkeeper, but he knew that the best way to spring answers from a quarry was to be unpredictable. He smiled.

''How fortunate that crash this evening came down in Sang Quarter rather than here. You have an attractive shop. It would be a pity to see it burn.''

Rafael's eyes widened slightly. He looked puzzled. Mentally Cocipec swore. The fat one was acting consummately.

''A crash, Mailord? Yes, it would be a—''

Cocipec turned away without allowing Rafael to finish. Rafael was too clever to be caught by his simple trickery. Cocipec longed to arrest the fat one and put him through the mind sieve, but there was no proof. His fist clenched at his side. There was never proof.

Snapping his fingers at his bodyguard, who cleared the doorway of the shop, Cocipec strode out, leaving Krilit to hurry after him with the fish sloshing in its bowl.

This time, Cocipec vowed, his agents would find the connection. If Earthers had infiltrated the city—and the very idea filled him with horrified fury—then they would have to make contact with traitors. If Rafael was one of those traitors, they would come to him. Cocipec grunted to himself. He would catch them. It was a matter of honor.

* * *

Kelly nearly walked past the shop and had to back up. He had expected a fish shop to be a place where fish were sold as food, not as pets, decorations, and gifts. Leaving 41 and Beaulieu outside, Kelly shouldered his way inside and looked about through the crowd for his contact.

The smell of emulsion, aquatic plants, and mingled perfume oils nearly overwhelmed him.

Rafael—easily recognizable from the AIA's data files—came hurrying up with annoyance visible on his face.

"This is a respectable business. You cannot afford my prices, hillman—"

"Sparrow," said Kelly softly in Glish.

Rafael's round face took on a yellow tinge. He rubbed his lips a moment, then glared at Kelly.

"No, I do not have spuro," he said loudly. "It is illegal to keep them in captivity. Only someone spawned in an *alley* would want to buy one. Go away. Go, before I call the troopers to throw you out."

Kelly stared at him a moment, then turned on his heel and strode from the shop. Looking startled, Beaulieu and 41 followed.

At the end of the block, Kelly plunged down a narrow side street into near darkness, wishing Salukans would provide better urban lighting, and began to hunt for the alley which must run behind the row of shops.

"Kelly," said Beaulieu in puzzlement, "what's going on? I thought you were supposed to be accepted as Rafael's cousin. Why did he throw you out?"

Kelly was wondering the same thing. He ran his hand along the damp, mossy wall. "Maybe there were too many people around. Who knows?" He stopped in frustration. "I thought he told me to come to the alley, but there isn't one back here."

"Was Rafael giving you a warning?" persisted Beaulieu as Kelly turned around and stared back the way they'd come. "Or didn't he recognize the signal?"

"He recognized it, all right." Kelly started walking again, heading back toward Stolat Road.

"There must be a trap if he warned you to get out," said 41.

Kelly's exploring hand plunged into a narrow crack. "Wait!" he said excitedly. "Stand between me and the main street."

Beaulieu and 41 complied. Kelly pulled out his torch and played its light along the space. About sixty centimeters, he estimated. The average human body could fit into a forty-five centimeter space. He frowned, not liking the idea of crawling sideways into such a narrow fissure, but it had to be what Rafael was referring to. Snapping off the torch, he dropped his gear on the ground and glanced at them.

"Keep watch. I'm going—"

"Commander, don't be a fool. We were told to abort this mission if the slightest thing went wrong. So far nothing is going right. If—"

"Dr. Beaulieu," said Kelly firmly. "I am going to explore this alley. Our job is to get Arnaht and his family out of Byiul, and a couple of small setbacks aren't enough to make me give up on that objective. They have as much right to freedom as we do, and we're going to try our very best to give them that. Am I clear?"

For a moment she was silent, then she said quietly, "Yes, Commander. Quite clear."

"Good. Now, keep alert," he said, and slid into the alley.

Alley was not the word for it. Crawl space perhaps. Crack. With his left hand groping along the wall ahead of him he crabbed along in total darkness, listening to his own breathing and trying not to flinch whenever his fingers crossed slime trails left by insects.

When he thought he had gone about far enough, he switched on his torch and played it carefully over the wall. Steel doors designed to recess into the wall permitted access into the various shops, but none of them seemed to be marked in any way. Frustrated, Kelly paused a moment and rested his forehead against the cold wall. It had been a long, tense day; he had a lot to accomplish yet; and he meant to help Arnaht defect, even if he had to bypass Rafael completely.

A soft click to his left brought him alert. Switching off his torch, he waited tensely in the darkness. A door rolled open and soft light spread out into the alley. Kelly squinted, aware that he had nowhere to hide. He hoped it was Rafael.

A silhouetted figure leaned out. Tensing, Kelly held his breath.

"Sparrow?" whispered a voice.

Kelly closed his eyes as he let out his breath. Quickly he scuttled to the door and slipped inside, blinking at the light within a stockroom cluttered with biodegradable crates, leaning stacks of fishbowls, a worktable supporting inventory records and a half-eaten meal congealed and abandoned. A strong, unpleasant odor of grain and stagnant water filled the air.

Rafael's immense bulk quivered beneath his black *chunta* as he rolled the door shut. He frowned at Kelly and gestured for him to be silent. Wheezing slightly, he threaded a path through the clutter and switched on a rotary fan.

Its hum was loud and constant, making a good noise cover for conversation. Kelly frowned as the breeze it created touched his face. He tried to imagine living his whole life under constant surveillance, with every word and action monitored. It would be hell.

"*Avi*," said Rafael, turning to face him. "You did well to come so quickly. Where—"

Kelly held up his hand. "First, can we base operations here or has something gone wrong?"

Rafael scowled. "That *kuprat* Cocipec from DUR came snooping tonight. I know he'll throw a surveillance net around me now. Tight, to choke me into making a mistake." Rafael closed his fist in illustration. "As for you . . . how did you bring down a military Sharpskeet? Now the authorities are stirred to great anger, and everything will be unsettled."

Kelly frowned, not liking the news that DUR was sniffing around. "What else is wrong?" he asked. "Sparrow hasn't backed out, has he?"

Impatience, perhaps even scorn, crossed Rafael's face. He dabbed at perspiration and shook his hand in negation. "DUR can sit outside and hear every word. It is a *net*, you see. They will—"

"We have equipment to counteract that," said Kelly. "No problem."

Rafael blinked, and he stared at Kelly with his mouth open. "So easy," he murmured. "Is everything easy for you Earthers? Propaganda tells us how protected we are, and yet here you have come in among us. An Alliance force could strike Gamael at any time and blast us to Shevul."

Kelly watched him with compassion, realizing that despite his political leanings Rafael must have never actually met a human face-to-face before. It took time to make the adjustment.

"It wasn't easy to get here," he said quietly. "We shot down that craft because it caught us at the city perimeter. One of my men is injured. A house-to-house search is being conducted in the area where we had to leave part of our equipment, and if that equipment is found we haven't much chance of getting offworld. Plus, our ship could be detected at any time."

Kelly drew a sharp breath. "But we're damned good at what we do, Rafael. Just as you are."

Rafael shook himself. "Yes, I understand. Welcome . . . I do not know your name."

"Commander Bryan Kelly of AIA Special Operations."

Rafael blinked. "The Space Hawks."

"That's right. Just call me Kelly."

"You and your men are welcome in my house, Kelly."

"Thanks." Kelly hesitated, then allowed himself to venture a grin. "Shall I give you my dagger? That is the custom for houseguests, isn't it?"

Rafael inclined his head. "You have studied us well. Keep your dagger. It is permitted among kinsmen, and you are to be my cousin. How many are there of you?"

Kelly thought of Caesar and Phila busy swimming along the bottom of Centime Canal if they were still on their schedule. "Just three," he said, "including myself."

Rafael frowned as though he had expected more. "Only three? How will—"

"They're waiting out in the street."

Rafael pursed his lips. "Very well. Upstairs, you will find

places prepared for you. I think you will be comfortable waiting there. Now I must go back to my last few customers and close the shop. It will take some time."

"Right," said Kelly, glancing toward the narrow stairs leading up to the next floor. "We also have work to do. When is the rendezvous with Sparrow?"

Rafael looked alarmed and cast an anxious glance at the fan. "Later," he said, sidling past Kelly. "All must be later."

"Hey!" said Kelly. "I want to know a few—"

But Rafael did not look back. He opened a door and vanished into the front of his shop. Kelly heard the sound of an electronic bolt engaging. Frustrated, Kelly stuck his head out into the alley and whistled softly.

In moments Beaulieu darted inside, followed by 41. Kelly shot him a look and was relieved to see his eyes clearer.

"Good, it's warm in here," said Beaulieu, rubbing her arms briskly. "We were ready to give up on you."

"Rafael is nervous," said Kelly. "He thinks DUR has snoops planted on the shop. The fan is his version of a jammer. Our quarters are upstairs."

41 frowned and drew his Brud & Marston .44, a short, big-bored percussion pistol that was ugly but effective. It had a barrel vented near the muzzle to soften its tendency for sloppy recoil. Heavier than a plasma weapon, its carbonite breech felt solid and stiff in the palm. It carried blunt-tipped slugs with lightweight jackets containing shot suspended in liquid gel. They were designed to fly at high velocity, smash into the target, and release the shot. Serious, damaging ammo that needed only one shot to kill. Perhaps too serious, but Kelly had selected the weapon for his squad because it didn't ricochet and it wouldn't penetrate walls if it missed its target. They had to use percussion weapons on this mission because Salukan sensors were calibrated to detect the electronic charge circuits built into standard-issue plasmas.

"No good exit," 41 said, glancing around. "We could be trapped up there if Rafael turns against us."

"He's proven loyal so far," said Kelly. "I'll set up the jammer. Doctor, you can recalibrate your medical scanner and check for snoops."

Beaulieu nodded. "Right."

Kelly met 41's gaze. "If you feel up to it, look for additional exits. We might as well get familiar with the layout of this place."

41 moved off like a cat on prowl.

"Did Rafael tell you when we're meeting Sparrow?" asked Beaulieu.

"Not yet."

She started to speak, but Kelly held up his hand. "Let's get to work. There's a lot to do."

"And he could be setting us up right now," she said nervously. "I think 41's right. This smells like a trap."

Kelly sighed. "Don't let your imagination get carried away. I don't think Rafael is double-crossing us. At least, let's not worry about that until we have to."

Reluctantly Beaulieu grinned. "Am I sounding paranoid?"

"Very."

She glanced at 41, who was threading his way across the cluttered storeroom. "Must be catching."

A blip on her scanner caught her attention. Kelly crowded close to look.

"Snoops everywhere," she said. "So thick I can't even isolate them. And Rafael uses a *fan* for interference?"

She and Kelly stared at each other.

"We'd better hope the jammer can handle it," he said at last.

"Put it on maximum power. Kelly?"

"Yes?"

"My paranoia is coming back."

3

*The hand extended in friendship can hold a dagger . . .
the kiss of thy wife, poison.*

—*School Manual,
teachings of Hithmal*

The Harvsk TR90 jammer squatted on its short tripod in the center of the floor, emitting a subliminal hum that grated on Kelly's nerves. He stood at the room's single wide window, which was closed now with wooden shutters against the cold air outside. Kelly opened one slat and stared out into the night at the low jumble of rooftops beneath a sky sprinkled with unfamiliar stars.

Behind Kelly, 41 stalked about, his feet soundless on beautiful woven carpets. Rafael's second-story living quarters ran the full length of the shop and consisted of an opulent bedchamber, a reception room for guests, and an elaborate food galley equipped with state-of-the-art appliances.

Turning away from the window, Kelly rubbed his eyes. They felt grainy with fatigue.

''Caesar and Phila should have checked in by now,'' he said worriedly.

Beaulieu stretched and sat down with a weary grunt. ''Nothing is going right,'' she grumbled. ''Maybe you'd better try calling them.''

41 made a noise of protest. Kelly stared regretfully at

his wristband and shook his head. "Not without alerting every surveillance unit in this sector. And with DUR prowling so close, even Caesar's pulse code transmission may register—"

The door burst open, startling Kelly and 41 into whipping around. Beaulieu jumped to her feet. But only Rafael entered, wheezing from his climb up the stairs. Behind him came the young boy who had been sweeping the shop.

Kelly swiftly wrapped the ends of his headdress about his face. "This is private, Rafael," he said in alarmed Saluk. "Between us alone."

"*Darshon a mei!*" snapped Rafael. He shoved the boy aside with enough force to make him stagger. The boy crouched and pressed his forehead to the floor. "You are my guest. How dare you tell me who may be in my house."

Kelly blinked and swiftly pulled himself back under control. "Forgive me," he said. "I have expressed myself poorly. But the fewer who know of our presence here, the better."

"*Suh,*" said Rafael. "The boy is a deaf-mute and half-witted besides. He understands nothing."

As he spoke, Rafael nudged the boy with his toe. The boy looked at him fearfully, inclined, and ran into the galley. Rafael walked up to the jammer and glared at it. "The room is hot. You should have turned on the fans. What is this?"

"Our jammer is neutralizing all the snoops," said Kelly, removing his headdress and tossing it onto a chair. "It's safe to talk."

Rafael turned on a pair of fans anyway, stirring up a powerful breeze that billowed his black *chunta* and made him look larger than ever. "A DUR monitor is hovering outside. We are all in jeopardy, Earther. If your presence becomes known—"

"It won't," said Kelly with equal irritation. "We are—"

But Rafael wasn't listening. "One session with the interrogators and we are all finished. Merciful Ru, what have I done to deserve this? Everything has been well with me until now. I make quiet, careful exchanges causing no suspicion. I have built a comfortable life for myself. And now that quaking coward Arnaht squeaks for help and you Earthers come for him without regard for the consequences. We could all be undone because of this. All of us! And when my entire network is caught and torn into pieces to decorate the outer walls of the Defended City, who will your Alliance have to spy upon the Empire?''

Kelly stared at him. ''How can you believe ideologically in the Alliance, work at risk to yourself against the oppression of your own government, and at the same time begrudge someone else the chance to enjoy the freedom the Alliance offers?''

Rafael pushed out his hands in a shrug, and the costly rings on his fat fingers glittered. ''What ideology? The Alliance pays me a fortune to be a traitor. Would I make as much from the Pharaon's treasury working as a civil servant?''

He came up to Kelly and stabbed a finger in Kelly's abdomen. ''Gold is my ideology, Earther. Not your stupid creditary banking system where little numbers are shoved around from one name to another, but gold that weighs heavy in my hand.'' He jabbed Kelly again. ''If the danger becomes too great, then I stop working for the Alliance. I might even change sides.''

Kelly didn't appreciate the threat. ''Look,'' he began angrily, ''I understand that the extra surveillance has upset you. But we know our job. We aren't going to jeopardize you.''

Rafael flung up his hands. ''I should never have involved myself in this. Defection . . . ridiculous. Arnaht would do better to walk into the desert and perish than to try to live among Earthers.''

''This is wasting time,'' said Kelly. ''I want to speak to Sparrow. Tonight. Now.''

Rafael's boy returned from the galley carrying a tray laden with food. Rafael pounced on a bowl of pink, globular fruit and popped one into his mouth.

''You can't,'' he said around it, chewing vigorously. ''The meeting time is set for tomorrow. It cannot be changed.''

Kelly pointed at the comm handset sitting upon a table. ''Call him. We don't need a rendezvous. He can be given his instructions from here and—''

''How many times must I explain?'' said Rafael. ''Curfew

is absolute. We are trapped in this house. The whole city is closed until dawn.''

''Then we'll meet at dawn,'' said Kelly. ''But in the meantime—''

Rafael selected another fruit and stuffed it into his mouth. A trickle of juice ran down his chin, and the boy wiped it for him. ''No. All has been arranged with care. You must work our way.''

With a noise of impatience, 41 pulled off his headdress and said, ''Your way is unimportant. Kelly, do you want me to make the call?''

Kelly never got to answer, for a horrified Rafael shoved his boy aside and pointed at 41.

''What is this creature? *Kos!* Get out of my dwelling!''

41 stiffened, and his golden eyes narrowed to slits. He advanced on Rafael.

Kelly stepped quickly between the two men. ''This is one of my operatives, Rafael. Your personal views on mixed races had better remain personal.''

Rafael stared at him as though he were crazy. ''Do you not understand the danger of a rogue-male?''

Kelly blinked and Rafael glared past him at 41. ''Living with Earthers, slaving for Earthers, trying to be an Earther. You know nothing of the hunter's moon or of blood-call, which is strong during Carnival. You have no control. You are dangerous.''

41's gaze burned into Rafael. ''Blood-call,'' he said with contempt. ''Will you next speak of vein-burn and the Terror of Walking Alone?''

None of it made any sense to Kelly. But Rafael's gaze widened. He breathed jerkily.

''Those are myths,'' said 41. ''You read too much of the old writings of your culture. How many blood-calls have *you* been forced to control?''

Rafael did not answer.

41's lips curled. He turned to Kelly. ''This one is a fool. He cannot be a warrior, and he hides his shame with these accusations. Let us be done with him.''

''No,'' said Kelly slowly. Rafael wasn't telling the truth,

and there was something dark in the back of 41's eyes that he didn't like. "We need him."

"How can you trust such a one?" asked Rafael. "They are used as spies, conditioned and set loose across the galaxy to be—"

"That's enough," snapped Kelly.

41's eyes flew to Kelly's and held them as though he suddenly feared Kelly would believe the fat man. "It has not been done. I would not betray you, Kelly."

In that naked moment Kelly saw the deep insecurity that always lay beneath 41's fierce facade. The insecurity that stemmed from having no family, from having no friends, from having no one to trust or to be trusted by. Kelly and the Hawks had offered him all that, but as yet 41 did not quite seem able to let himself depend on it.

Kelly reached out and clasped 41's shoulder. "I know."

"Touching, but it proves nothing," said Rafael. "You are a product of—"

Without warning, 41 seized the fat man's throat and pressed the muzzle of his Brud into the softness of Rafael's upper chest.

"Keep speaking, fat one," he said softly, "and I will kill you."

Rafael gulped and rolled his eyes at Kelly. "You let him threaten me like this? You do not command him?"

"I command him," said Kelly. He'd had his fill of Rafael. "And I don't blame him. Let him go, 41."

41 released Rafael and stalked into the galley with angry disdain.

Kelly glanced at Beaulieu. In silence, she hurried after 41.

As soon as the door closed behind them, Rafael sagged, but Kelly wasn't through with him.

"That was stupid," he snapped. "All Alliance personnel are checked out thoroughly."

Rafael raised his plump hands angrily. His rings flashed in the light. "So you say. Does he have an excellent background and good credentials of every kind? Or is there nothing to say where he came from?"

Kelly started to answer, then fell silent. His eyes narrowed thoughtfully.

"Yes," said Rafael with a sneer. "I am not such a paranoid fool as you think. I would not want that creature guarding my back."

"I trust him," said Kelly stubbornly.

"Oh, he may not betray you here. Perhaps not for months or years. Who knows what will trigger his conditioning?"

Unwillingly Kelly remembered West's reservations about 41. He frowned, hating the prejudice in Rafael that had planted this seed of doubt.

"You have been warned," said Rafael. "And I can see you do not like my warning. But I tell you this, Earther. It was meant kindly."

"Thanks," said Kelly. "But I still trust him."

Rafael pushed out his hands in a shrug. "Trust him as you please, but as for me, I shall sleep with a dagger in my fist tonight."

4

Children are as pools of water. Their strength is an old man's joy. Their laughter is graven upon his heart.
—from the Scroll of Tees

Melaethia had never ridden in a litter before. It skimmed the air upon a grav-flat, with four armed bearers to guide it to its destination and to guard her safety among the night revelers. The sides and roof were heavily polarized for protection against the hot sun; tonight, she saw only vague shadows and distorted lights. She would like to see Carnival. She would like to jump down from the litter and run into the laughing crowds. She would like to drink hot copra and smell fresh blood. She would like to dance until dawn.

But she was no longer a child. She had gained importance and she lived within the Defended City. The steward of the Pharaon's household had chosen her as a potential future concubine. She spent long days in school, learning the arts of pleasure: how to enhance her beauty with the most artful cosmetics, how to perfume her hair and skin, how to glide when she walked, how to dance as though the soles of her feet rode the air, how to make a man laugh within his bed.

Aware of the honor that could be hers, she worked hard to master everything she was taught. But always inside her heart there lay fear like a serpent coiled.

For the Pharaon was God made mortal, and few ever saw him. Law forbade any to look directly at his face.

The Third Court of Women—none of whom had ever been with him—was rife with talk and rumor. Their favorite tale was of a young maiden so pure and delicate she could not endure the touch of the sun upon her skin. She had great beauty and delighted the eye of Nefir, but when he lay with her she caught fire and perished of his greatness.

The older ones, nearly past their prime and knowing they would never be called now to the First Court of Women, would exchange glances and say, "Melaethia looks so much like her. They could be sisters. Do you fear catching fire, child?"

She didn't believe such a simple folk story, of course. But although she pretended great composure, she was afraid. Afraid of what she might do or say in an unguarded moment, afraid that whim might turn Nefir against her, afraid that she might care for him.

The Pharaon was a tyrant. He had absolute power. He ruled an empire of ninety planets from within his walls. Only a chosen few of his subjects ever saw him, but he was feared by all. No one dared question his orders, ever. No one dared speak out against his edicts, however harsh. There was one law within the Empire, and it was Nefir's will.

Melaethia's father had taught her that such great power was a terrible corruption, an evil thing that twisted the men who possessed it. Arnaht taught her tolerance and gave her an open mind. In the protection of her father's home, she could discuss any subject she pleased and speak any opinion she pleased without fear of reprisal.

Yet he had always warned her to conceal her opinions in public. Free speech was not permitted. Certain criticisms could lead to arrest.

Sometimes she resented her father for making her aware of injustices that she could not change.

Worst of all, having taught her to dislike the Pharaon, her father nevertheless showed great pride in her placement within the Defended City.

"Theory and reality," he said when she accused him of

deceiving her. "The real world versus the ideal world. I'm sorry I have taught you so much, and yet someday you will teach your child to think and act independently. And that child will teach its own."

He had said that to her almost two years ago. Now, riding along in what might be her last visit home, she could smile over the pathetic smallness of his vision. Billions of subjects belonged to the Empire. Her children would be as a grain of sand among them, ineffectual and unheard.

The litter bumped gently to the ground. Knuckles rapped upon the side.

"We have arrived, dama."

Melaethia put aside her thoughts and emerged from the litter. She wore a heavy *sulla*, a thickly woven traveling cloak fitted with a hood and mask that covered her completely. No man save those within her family could look upon her. If ever she went in to serve Nefir's pleasure, even her own father could never gaze upon her face again.

She shivered.

To her right, Centime Canal shimmered black beneath the reflections of the globe lanterns strung along the bank. Beyond it rose the mighty walls of the Defended City. Tall towers within the compound twinkled with lights.

The security inspector made her pause at the doors while he ran a scanner over her. Allowed to pass on, she left her bearers outside and took a lift up to the fourth and top floor . . . home.

Her brother Dausal opened the door for her. Impeccable in his fawn uniform of the 12th Lancers cadet corps, his rank sash glittering with his latest commendation, he stood shoulders and head above her. He did not smile in greeting. He never did.

Melaethia sighed and took off the *sulla*. Beneath it she wore a simple gown clasped at the shoulder with a brooch of worked gold. It fell in straight pleated folds to the floor, leaving her arms bare except for the modest circlet of gold wire about her left wrist. Her head felt loose inside her new wig, which was looped elaborately and braided with strands of gold.

"Where's *pata*?" she asked.

Dausal's black eyes narrowed. He glanced over his shoulder, showing her his chiseled profile with its ridged cheekbones and narrow jaw. "In there, putting the last touches to his feast. I'm to keep you here until he is ready. Do you want copra?"

She hesitated. "Who made it?"

"I did." Dausal sounded irritated. "This is a study night, Melaethia. He knows I don't have time during the week to come for these affairs."

Dausal was always in a hurry, burning with ambition. He had no time for family, and it took a filial command to bring him home.

"Do you want a drink or not?"

"Of course," she said softly, lowering her gaze from his handsome, angry face. "I always like the way you make it."

"Suh," he said, turning away to a large bowl of beaten silver sitting upon an inlaid cupboard. He ladled her a cupful of the smoking liquid, allowing the ladle handle to clatter against the bowl.

When he turned to thrust the cup at her, dark color burned in his cheeks. "So you have learned to practice your seductive wiles on any man, even your own brother."

Her gaze flew up to his in startlement. "No," she said in dismay. "I—"

"Take it," he said roughly, making sure her fingers did not touch his as she took the cup from him.

His anger made her shrink to the other side of the foyer. She bent her face over the steaming cup and sipped, taking refuge in its scalding spices. Her throat ached with the effort to hold back an attempt to reason with him.

"What is taking the old man so long?" fumed Dausal, pacing past her, then back again, filling the small space with his fierce energy.

"Have you quarreled again with him?"

"No!"

She flinched, and even he seemed to realize the extent of his vehemence. For a moment his eyes softened and he was not a rigid monster in uniform but her younger brother.

"In three days I report to the Temple of Geurs, to offer my warrior vows."

Emotion rose inside her, filling her throat, burning at the back of her eyes. She stared at him and understood at last.

Geurs, the god of war. In that ancient arena somewhere on the plain between Byiul and the Menieth space port, officers took their oaths of allegiance to Pharaon and Empire. Cadets such as Dausal performed the rite of passage that made them officially men. She was not allowed to see it, but she'd heard enough to know it was dangerous. Dausal could be killed.

All of his fighting skills would be tested to the utmost. If not killed, he could be maimed for life. If he survived intact, he would go into the army.

To prepare for this test meant a strict regiment of exercise, drill, and meditation. It also meant chastity. Lifting her eyes, Melaethia studied him from her new knowledge as a courtesan and saw the nervousness bottled up inside him with no outlet for release. By driving himself this way he walked the edge of blood-call.

Small wonder he could not endure her presence, since she exuded sexuality.

Arnaht had chosen a poor time for a dinner feast. Yet, when? In a few days Dausal would be posted away to his new commission and she might be closed within the Defended City forever.

"My children. Welcome, both of you."

Arnaht stood in the doorway of the reception room, beaming at them with his arms stretched wide. Melaethia glided over to embrace him. His loose, undyed houserobe scratched her supple skin.

Something was wrong. Arnaht's back muscles beneath his robe were tense when she patted him. His face wore too determined a smile.

"Ah . . ." He inhaled deeply. "What a delightful fragrance. Like a thousand flowers in the room. Is she not lovely, my son?"

"Yes!" snapped Dausal, his black eyes as deep as space. "She is . . . lovely. She should not be here tonight. You know that."

Arnaht's smile faded. "I know it," he said quietly. "It could not be helped."

"Why?" asked Melaethia, ready to lighten the conversation. "Are we celebrating something? I smell banans. The Master of the Baths would have a fit if he knew that. They are so very fattening, and I don't care!"

Laughing, she slipped past her father and entered the reception room. Tall-ceilinged and kept strictly for the entertaining of guests, it was furnished with dark old chairs from the eastern region of Signes, woven rugs, and curved brass hooks for ancient globe lanterns. These things had been part of her mother's dowry. The room itself smelled of childhood: waxed wood, fragrances of floor oil and *frangzini*, tempting scents from the food.

A table had been set up by the tall windows now closed with wooden shutters. All of their favorite dishes from childhood had been prepared. She picked up covers and exclaimed in wonder.

"It really is a feast. *Pata*, what are you up to? What do you have to tell us?"

She spoke in jest, thinking he must have been promoted to a higher position in the Ministry of Information. To her surprise, he frowned and looked suddenly worried. But before she could speak, he pointed to their eating couches and they dutifully bowed their heads in memory of his wife and their mother, dead these eight years.

"*Pata,*" began Melaethia as he handed her a dish of banans. "What are you—"

"Later," he said with a smile, evading her eyes. "Eat. This is an occasion. And I want no talk of diets or fasting from either of you. Eat."

When the meal was done, however, and Melaethia could not swallow another morsel, she licked the sweet stickiness from her fingers and stretched upon her couch.

"A concubine died today in childbirth," she said. "Rumors within the court are that a replacement will be chosen soon. She was not a favorite; there will be no mourning and no slaves killed in her honor."

She saw Arnaht's bony hand clench hard upon a cushion. But it was Dausal who spoke.

"You want to be that replacement, do you not?"

All afternoon she had imagined this conversation and rehearsed her answer. Now, however, she hesitated. "I don't know. I thought I did when there was no chance of it. But now I . . . The steward of the households came twice today, but it is rare for a selection to be made from the Third Court. Usually only the Second Court can be . . ."

Aware that she was babbling, she let her voice trail off.

Silence deepened around her. She dared not look at either of them. There was pain in her heart, overlaid by that same burst of excitement every time she thought about being chosen by Nefir.

Drawing a breath, she forced herself to glance at her father. "Well?" she said.

He rose from his couch without meeting her eyes. "The room has grown hot," he said.

He turned on the fans, filling the room with a low hum. It gave Melaethia time to sit erect on her couch and straighten her gown. She kept smoothing the folds over and over, trying not to be angry. He need not make her feel ashamed. She had no talent for the arts, or athletics, or science. Her only asset lay in her beauty and that was a gift of genetics. Arnaht was a burean of middle position. He was descended from a minor house on both sides. No marriage had been arranged for her; what other future did she have? What did he expect of her?

When he returned to the table, however, he did not speak of the Pharaon.

"I have spent all day considering my words. There seems no way to say this." He paused a moment, gazing at them each in turn. "I can no longer endure my life here. My work, my existence, are meaningless to me. I am strangling."

"What? I don't understand," said Dausal. "Are you ill?"

"No." Arnaht smiled sadly. "I am going to defect to the Alliance."

"What?" Dausal rushed to his feet. Color surged into his face and he clenched his fists. Somehow he managed to keep

his voice lower than the hum of the fans. "Are you mad? Do you know what you are saying?"

"Why, *pata*?" broke in Melaethia, feeling numb from the shock.

"You know why. You know my . . . private views."

"Darshon!" swore Dausal, sweeping dishes off the table with a mighty crash. "Your views are a shame to all of us. This whole thing is absurd. There is no way to leave—"

"Suppose there was," said Arnaht eagerly. "Suppose I had a way to freedom. Would you come with me? Would you, Dausal? Would you, Melaethia?"

"Yes," she said. "I would come."

Dausal turned on her. "Fool! You'd say anything to please him. It's impossible."

"No," said Arnaht. "Alliance agents are here in the city, waiting to take us out."

"It can't be done. The city is protected. No unauthorized entry or exit—"

"Ahe, Dausal. Don't spout regulations at me. I know them all," said Arnaht. "They found a way to get in. And they're waiting. I must contact them soon. That's why I summoned you here tonight. You must decide if you want to come."

"Never!" said Dausal hotly, pacing about the room. "You should go to a physician and be checked. Too much sun—"

"Stop it," said Melaethia. "He isn't crazy. You know that. Denying what he is saying won't help matters."

Dausal threw her an exasperated glance. "Yes, but *listen* to him. We are at the center of the Empire, protected by the most sophisticated means. No one can get in or out. Yet our dear *pata* here claims that he has decided to defect and therefore help has miraculously materialized. Impossible."

"Not," said Arnaht slowly, "if you consider I have been giving classified information to the Alliance for nearly seventeen years."

Dausal's bronzed face paled to a sickly yellow. Melaethia rose to her feet, staring at her father in disbelief. How could this be? He could not be telling them the truth.

Yet she knew her father did not lie.

Implications swam through her mind. She exchanged glances with Dausal, seeing her shock mirrored in his eyes.

"Then it isn't theory," she said, groping for words. "Is it?"

"No, child," Arnaht said gently.

Dausal took a step forward, then back up as though he did not trust himself. "Did *masere* know?" he asked.

Arnaht shook his hands. "It never seemed right to tell her. She was so proud of coming from a major house."

"You have shamed us," whispered Dausal. "We are stained forever."

"My son—"

"No!" shouted Dausal. "I am not your son! I could not belong to such a—to such a *traitor*. You should be turned in immediately."

He looked around for the handset. Melaethia ran to him.

"Dausal, you mustn't! He is our father. You can't have him arrested."

Dausal shook off her hand. "You would share his shame, I suppose. Do you feel proud to have a traitor for a father?"

"Don't call him that!"

"And what other term would you have?"

She felt her cheeks burning. Shame and anger warred within her.

Dausal seized her wrist and shook her, making her cry out. "He used to make us sit through his disgusting lectures, and you would nod, drinking in every word he said. You have become as bad as he is, liberal and softheaded. Look where it ends, sister! In Godinye—"

"*No!* He mustn't go there. He mustn't." Horror made her cling to Dausal as though she could physically hold him from acting. "Dausal, don't report him. Please."

"Why shouldn't I?"

She lifted brimming eyes to his black ones, seeing the hurt in him, the confusion running rampant through his guts as though a stave had been thrust in and was twisting.

"Because," she said, "it would destroy you."

He wrenched free and turned his back to her. His shoulders were shaking. She faced Arnaht in rage of her own.

"Go, then," she said furiously. "Go to your Earther friends and leave us be."

Arnaht's face looked as though a thousand years had been etched into it. "My child, I cannot. You are the pride of my loins. I can't abandon you."

She blinked. "You don't expect us to defect with you?"

"A moment ago you said you would come with me."

"Yes, but I . . . I didn't think. I . . ." She glanced away from him with a frown. To live the rest of her life as a criminal, condemned by her own kind? To live among *Earthers*? She shuddered. "We have our own lives. We are grown now."

"Grown, but not safe." He took her hands in his. "Melaethia, consider the law. You and Dausal would have to pay for my crimes. I can't leave you to that. Your only chance of safety is to come with me."

Her mouth went dry. She had not considered the consequences. It was happening too fast.

"But where would we go? How could we live with them? They are so strange, so repulsive."

Behind her Dausal snorted. "You've never seen one in your life."

"I have in the holos," she retorted. "What is the difference?"

"In real life they smell and they like to melt their enemies into puddles—"

"That's enough!" said Arnaht. "Both of you are reacting with your emotions. Think rationally about this."

"How?" said Dausal, his voice raw. "What is rational about any of it? I must return to the barracks. Curfew will sound soon. I—"

Melaethia pulled away from her father and ran to Dausal as he strode toward the door. "Please," she said urgently. "Please."

He paused with his hand upon the door. For a moment he looked at her and his face twisted with anguish. "What does he expect of me?" he whispered. "I'm an officer. My duty demands that I—"

"What of familial duty?" She gripped his hand, feeling

the calluses upon his fingers, the knobby ridges above his vestigial claws. "Dausal, it will tear you apart."

He jerked free of her. "He has ruined everything. My career, my life, my pride. I no longer have a father. I was spawned by *nothing*."

With a slam of the door he was gone. Grieving, Melaethia rubbed her burning eyes and turned back to Arnaht. He stood like graven stone in the center of the room, the broken dishes at his feet, the breeze from the fans billowing his houserobe.

"I did not want it to be like this," he said, his voice broken and old. "I did not want to lose him like this. My son. My son!"

It was a keening cry. Melaethia ran to him and enfolded him in her arms, rocking him in comfort he would not take. His arms remained rigid at his sides, but his face burrowed against her shoulder.

"My son," he whispered. "I have lost my son. I could have slit his throat and felt no worse."

"You have me, *pata*," she said soothingly. "I remain with you. I have said I will go with you and I will. You have me with you always."

His face was hot against her skin. "I know, daughter. But it is not the same."

She went home in the litter, her bearers running ahead of curfew. The *sulla* shielded her as she sat tensely rocking herself in resentment and humiliation.

There were always too many women; there were never enough warriors. It was the way of life that sons be prized above daughters. Still, the hurt ran deep.

She knew her father loved her. He had clung to her all the more desperately after Dausal left. With difficulty she had persuaded him to let her return to the Defended City tonight. She had promised to return to his apartment tomorrow afternoon as soon as she got permission from her keeper. But if she did not sleep tonight within the Third Court of Women, suspicion at her absence would be aroused.

Now that her shock was fading, it was exciting to think of leaving the Empire and seeing how other cultures lived.

Someone had once told her that women of the Alliance were not bound to state-ordained careers or arranged marriages. They worked beside men and did as they pleased.

Would she be allowed to do that?

The holos of Earther men were pale, short creatures, made upside down with a soft abdomen and a hard chest. Their necks were oddly flexible, letting their heads bob about queerly.

Tomorrow she would meet one.

She sat within the litter as it entered the Defended City, and could scarcely breathe.

The keeper of the Third Court berated her sharply for returning so late.

"My father is very ill," she replied to the rebuke. "I had to stay as long as I could."

Curfew sounded over the city, faint beyond the walls. Frosty air made her shiver as she scurried through the bathing rooms and into her quarters, where the other girls sat up in bed and jeered insults.

"Silence!" shouted the keeper, and extinguished the lights.

Darkness plunged over Melaethia's body, hiding her blushes from their prying eyes. Silence after lights was an absolute rule. Someone giggled, muffled into her pillow. There were rustlings, but Melaethia was safe from questions until dawn.

She unclasped her gown and let it fall to her feet. Beneath it she wore nothing. Climbing into her narrow bed, she snuggled beneath the warm duvet and lay there for several minutes.

Sleep refused to come. Her whole body tingled with enervation. There was too much to think about. Too much to wonder.

And then the idea came to her.

She gasped into her pillow, shocked at her own daring. But the idea would not be banished. It grew in her mind.

Someday you'll teach your children what I have taught you.

If she lived among the Earthers, she would never bear children. She had heard that sometimes an Earther and a Saluk mated. That was an abhorrence to her, something filthy which her whole being shied from.

Who, then, would she teach? Who would profit from the lesson of her freedom?

It was her fertile time. She slipped her hand furtively down her body, feeling the heat of her own skin. Dausal had known from her scent.

Poor Dausal . . . she could not think of him, for that would reawaken the pain cleaving her heart.

But her fertility would be wasted. She would live a barren life unless . . .

No, she did not dare. It was unthinkable. She would be caught. She might be killed.

But if she succeeded, the sacrifice of leaving Gamael would mean something.

Time crept by while she waited, listening to the breathing of her classmates, making certain no one else lay awake to catch her. Then at last she left her bed and picked up her gown. Making no sound in her bare feet upon the cold stone floor, she slipped from the room.

Even the keeper had retired to her quarters and did not prowl about as she sometimes did. Melaethia paused in the muted glow of light shining through the passageway and started to put on her gown. It was crumpled and she frowned. No one would let her get all the way to the Court of Delight dressed like this.

There was very little time, for the Pharaon would retire soon. She hurried to the baths and drew out a jeweled box containing the most costly unguents. Oiling her skin until she was all fragrance, she opened clothes chests and found a gown of scarlet layered sheer upon sheer with so many folds that it ceased to be transparent. Over it she shrugged on an open blue robe crusted with heavy gold embroidery that made it very heavy. Such rich garments had only one special purpose. She dug through the chest, ignoring the jewelry except for a head net of dangling pearls which she fitted on instead of a wig.

She should have painted her face, but there was not time and the light shining from the passageway outside the baths was too poor. Picking up a face shield, she slipped outside.

In the distance she heard musicians still playing and the

faint sound of laughter. The Pharaon kept late evenings, especially during Carnival. An opera composed in his honor was being performed tonight. When it finished, he would eat and then retire.

Breathless, she quickened her steps. As part of their training they had to know every aspect of what he liked and did not like.

He did not like surprises. Her heart thudded faster.

The loggia rustled with plant fronds swayed by the cold night air. Beyond, the curve of gardens lay dappled by golden moonlight. The musky fragrance of jessisine vine filled the air. Inhaling deeply, she reached the end of the loggia and put her hand upon the door.

The guard on the other side glared at her in sleepy surprise, then hastily averted his eyes as she raised the face shield.

"No one is permitted through this door, dama."

Her mouth was so dry she feared she would not be able to speak. Somehow she forced out the words: "I have been sent for."

The guard frowned in swift suspicion. "Where is the keeper? Where is your escort? The steward should be—"

"I have been sent for," she said again, unable to think of a more plausible lie. "Will you keep me here on your own authority?"

She bribed him with a pearl and he stepped back with a shrug. Girls occasionally slipped out. If caught with a man, they were beheaded. Not caring what he thought, Melaethia hastened on.

The next guard also took a bribe. She threaded her way through corridors, ducking out of sight whenever she encountered anyone. Eventually she pushed upon a door and found herself in an unlit antechamber hung with stifling, musty tapestries.

Someone else waited here. Melaethia heard a rustle and swift intake of breath. Face-to-face in the darkness, they stood in silence a moment.

"I was called," whispered a sultry voice in fury. "If that wretched eunuch wants to play political games with my keeper, he can think again."

Melaethia's face was burning. Desperately she kept her wits. If this concubine had been called for by name, her own ploy was hopeless.

"My name is sweeter upon the Excellency's lips," Melaethia whispered back.

"Speshie!" snapped the other, shocking Melaethia with her gutter insult. "You haven't been named any more than I have. You are Second Court if anything, no better than me. Go back and tell your keeper to pick another night. This one is mine."

"I'll give you a pearl," said Melaethia.

The other laughed. "I have many pearls. Silly fool, are you so drenched in that cheap scent you can't smell my fertility? The seer says I shall be a son's mother. If I bear Nefir a son, I shall wear pearls every day in the First Court."

"I'll give you my entire head net," said Melaethia recklessly, aware of its costly worth. "I am not fertile. I can't jeopardize your chances." She pulled off the net and held it out.

The other hesitated until Melaethia's nerves were snapping, then she snatched it from Melaethia's hand and rushed from the antechamber as though she feared Melaethia would change her mind and want it back.

Melaethia drew in a deep breath. She was shaking from nerves; her legs felt weak. Nefir would know as soon as he touched her that she had never been with him. If that angered him, she would die. He had killed women in his bed before—not with immortal fire, but with his own dagger. It was forbidden for her to leave her own court without permission, forbidden to present herself like this, forbidden to dare.

She spread wide her fingers to dry the dampness between them. Think of the arts, she told herself. Think of all you know about seduction. Blind him, entice him, make him give you a child.

Pregnancy was a difficult process. During the five months of term, she would grow breasts and the birth sac would swell large. She would be unable to walk, becoming totally helpless and dependent. Would the Earthers know how a Saluk baby was born? Their way must be so very different. Would they kill her with their ignorance?

Stop thinking.

She heard a noise through the walls, and her whole body grew cold. A tap upon the door startled her. She jumped back, staring while her heart pounded. Then slowly, with unsteady hands, she opened it and entered the bedchamber.

Dim light globes cast no more than a glimmer of illumination. A translucent floor of pale pink alabaster glowed like alien flesh. Washbowls of gold with jeweled ewers waited upon carved stands. Heated air swirled gently about her ankles. A valet, wearing the red sash of a eunuch, bustled about straightening the room and plumping the cushions upon the bed.

Melaethia stared. The bed hangings stretched all the way to the ceiling far overhead. Embroidery of gold and silver glistened in the light so that it all shimmered.

The valet brushed past her. ''Give me your robe.'' He pulled it from her shoulders. ''Sit on that chair and wait. He'll be here soon. Don't move, and if you steal anything, I'll cut off your hand.''

She sat, keeping her face behind the shield. After a moment he left, and silence surrounded her.

With difficulty she swallowed and tried to use meditation to prepare herself. She had to be calmer or she could please no one.

A murmur of voices and laughter outside brought her to her feet. A door in the distance was thrown open, and she heard Nefir enter. The pattern of his speech, fast then slow, laughing through words, a yelp as his ceremonial clothing was removed. The babble of courtiers.

Melaethia felt as though she were burning alive. She swiftly pulled off layer after layer of her gown, following an instinct that told her he was too keyed up to watch dancing. He might be drunk, but he would want instant compliance.

By the time the inner doors opened and he swept through with a spill of bright light like a mantle upon his shoulders, Melaethia wore only a single, gossamer layer. The breeze of his entry billowed the transparent cloth against the contours of her body.

Nefir stopped and gazed at her. "Well, well," he said in a voice so deep it rumbled inside her. "The steward selects infants now."

The courtiers laughed dutifully and bowed themselves out at Nefir's negligent gesture.

They stood alone with the doors bolted all around. Nefir picked up a goblet and drank deeply. He was tall and rangy of build with a silk houserobe shimmering from his shoulders.

"No paint to make you look older. No jewelry to clash and clatter. No wit or no voice. Can you speak?"

She dropped her eyes. "Yes, Excellency."

"A pleasing voice." He walked closer and she felt suffocated. "Your simplicity reminds me of my High Consort when I wed her. Good. I am weary of wit. It has filled my ears all night. I have stared at dancers until I feel blind. I have heard music until my ears are numb. You do not sing?"

"No, Excellency."

He touched her cheek, using a hint of claw to force her to look at him. She shivered as their eyes met. His were twilight blue, flecked with silver and green. He smiled, drawing back his lips all the way to his fangs.

"Have you a name, little one?"

"Melaethia," she whispered.

"Song of the wind. Very pretty." His fingers ran down her skin to her throat. They tightened there, pressing hard upon the cartilage. A burst of pleasure went through her, much greater than when the instructor had touched her in that way.

She dared move closer as his claws dug in. Her scent released, flooding them, and she heard his sharp intake of breath.

"Come to bed, little one," he murmured.

Even so, she was not sure she would please him until he gave her the first bite. Then she forgot her instructions, forgot her fear, forgot everything except him and the vicious ecstasy of blood-call.

5

When the moon turns blood-yellow, beware thy neighbor and double-bar thy doors. It is hunting season, and all is fair game.

—ancient Salukan saying

Spirou Canal curved around the east side of the Defended City. Forty meters wide and four fathoms deep, its dirty waters rumbled with the wake of heavy service traffic crisscrossing its surface. The whole canal network of Byiul was simple. It consisted of Spirou and Centime, which encircled the Defended City like two arms. Then there was an access canal which served to channel water brought down from the mountains on aqueducts into the city and a square of smaller canals circuiting Royal and Umle quarters.

Feeling as though he had swum along every inch of the whole network, Caesar shone his underwater torch through the murky silt and finally found the grille they'd been hunting along the foundation of the palace walls for the past hour.

In excitement he tapped Phila's shoulder and pointed. She nodded and together they swam upward to the grille where the force of churning water feeding into the canal swept Caesar sideways and back out into the current. Phila clung like a limpet to the grille and gestured at him to hurry.

Grumbling mentally, he returned. He withdrew his cutters from the gear bag tied to his belt and set to work.

The grille had been wrought of old metal, very stout and noncorroded. Concentrating on keeping the laser-thin plasma beam slicing at a precise angle, Caesar wondered why the devil these wig-heads couldn't use conventional open-gridded forcefields. Those were a snap to short-circuit. But this stuff came from the Dark Ages.

The plasma beam slipped and Caesar swore around his mouthpiece. Phila held on to his leg to keep him steady against the downsweep of current, and Caesar finished making the final cuts in the metal grille. Stowing his cutters, he gave Phila a thumbs-up sign and pulled the grille free. It dropped from sight into the murky bottom of the canal approximately three fathoms beneath them.

Caesar found himself sweating inside his wet suit. The grille was at the one-fathom mark, much closer to the surface than he'd expected. He felt exposed. A random energy probe could slice through the water to a depth of three meters at any time. The fact that so far one hadn't did little for his jumpy nerves.

He tapped Phila on the shoulder and made hand signals in the wavering light, warning her to watch the sharp ends of the grille so that she didn't tear her wet suit or her airhose as she swam through.

She nodded, small and shadowy in the backwash of the powerful halogen torch she carried.

Caesar went through first, kicking strongly against the force of the current draining into the canal and bracing himself with his hands to make sure he didn't snag.

Whoever had told their sources that the grille would be two fathoms deep was an idiot. Searching for it had not only taken time, but it had also depleted their oxygen supply. They were way off schedule and still not in position.

Sweat trickled down Caesar's face, and his mask began to fog again. He swore mentally. This underwater gear must have come from a museum. It was hotter than a thermal suit and fragile. He much preferred the up-to-date force-belt that created a flexible blister of environment. With it, all that was required was a lightweight oxygen pack strapped to the chest, with no hoses or tanks or face masks to fool with. But a force-belt would trigger the energy probe.

He'd heard the lab gang was coming up with a method of getting the human body to extract oxygen from water so that no environmental support was necessary at all. That sounded great in theory, but Caesar wasn't sure he wanted to breathe water. Anyway, the body couldn't take it for more than ten minutes without going into severe reaction spasms, so here they were in granny-gear, creeping along in constant danger of losing their air supply.

Phila handed him the torch and swam through the opening like an eel. Caesar shone the torch ahead of them. They found themselves inside a tunnel now, leading—he hoped—straight beneath the Defended City. He swam up, thinking he might be able to surface, but his outstretched hand touched the roof without any airspace.

Damn. If it was like this all the way through, they might as well go home.

Phila tugged on his ankle and pointed. Caesar dropped to about the middle of the tunnel and started swimming. About six meters in, the strength of the current lessened until it was barely noticeable. Caesar was glad, for his legs felt rubbery with exhaustion. He kept telling himself that this was *not* the palace sewer.

About seventy meters along they came to another grille. It was lighter weight than the first. Caesar cut through it quickly.

On the other side the tunnel narrowed. Again Caesar swam upward. This time he surfaced in about thirty centimeters of airspace.

He spat out his mouthpiece and sucked in some real air. It smelled unbelievably foul. Phila bobbed up beside him. She tended to tread water like a dog, using all four limbs instead of just her legs. The way she bobbed up and down, Caesar kept expecting her to sink completely under, but somehow she never did.

"This looks good," she gasped, shoving up her face mask to the top of her shaven head. She had a tiny, knobby skull, and without her customary mop of black curls, her dark eyes looked enormous.

Throughout his randy life Caesar had managed to find something appealing in just about every female he met, but women who were as bald as cue balls gave him the willies. He felt sorry for Phila, having to be disguised like this when, if everything went well, no wig-head would even see them at all. She knew it, and his pity made her mad at him.

All business, she continued tersely, "We should be beyond the walls. I think this ought to be position one. Do you want to call Kelly from here, or wait until position two?"

"Let's wait." Caesar tried a grin on her; she didn't smile back. "We're so far behind I hate to tell him we've only planted one device."

"Right," she said, floating her gear bag on the surface and getting out a flat, black rectangular box the length of her hand. She peered at it to be sure she had the correct serial sequence. "Steady me."

Caesar grabbed her small waist and boosted her so that she could adhere the snoop to the stone roof. The blocks were slick with moss. The snoop slid and Phila nearly dropped it in the water.

"Damn!"

"Watch out, will you?" Caesar's head went under. He juggled her, spitting out water. It tasted as bad as the air smelled. He tried not to think about poisonous microorganisms.

"It's not going to stick to this goop," she said impatiently. "Turn loose."

She dug about in her gear bag and found a tube of adhesive which she smeared across the bottom of the snoop. "This will do it."

Caesar watched doubtfully. "What if the water level rises and lowers? It could be washed off."

"This stuff will stick to anything, even wet slime," she said. "Boost."

She was right. It did stick. Caesar frowned at it a moment, waiting for it to fall off. When it didn't, he grinned. When he and Phila got through, the Defended City would have so many snoops crisscrossing underneath it the Pharaon wouldn't be able to go to the head without someone in AIA knowing about it.

Still grinning, Caesar paddled on, keeping his head above

the surface to conserve air supply. After all, they still had to get back.

Their next stop came at the junction where the tunnel forked. The ceiling angled more sharply here, rising perhaps a meter and a half above their heads. Large irregular patches of a sickly white fungus glowed dully after the light shone on them. Sounds carried on the water, echoing back hollowly.

While Phila smeared adhesive to her second snoop, Caesar studied the slope of the roof and decided to leave an explosive with a long-range circuit detonator—just in case HQ ever decided to give the Pharaon a little surprise.

Phila grabbed a rung bolted to the wall and used it to pull herself up within reach of the ceiling. A small square grate was just above it. She placed the snoop near the grate and let herself drop back into the water.

"Are you ready to call Kelly now?" she asked.

"Yeah, I guess." Caesar paddled to the wall and braced his elbow against it while he started sending a pulse-coded message over his comm.

The signal was set on a minute pip frequency that shouldn't arouse any notice, but these wig-heads were a paranoid bunch with more surveillance than anything he'd ever seen. He didn't want them catching his message coming out of these tunnels, so he kept it short:

"In place. Working hard."

Then he waited while Phila swam a short distance down the right tunnel, then came back and explored the left tunnel. Her torchlight caught eerie reflections off the oily surface of the water.

He stared at his shriveled fingers, still dyed blue as part of his disguise as a Yllrian. The water level was rising. He caught a rung and pulled himself a bit higher. After what seemed forever, he felt the tiny pulses on his wrist that marked Kelly's reply. Something splashed about then, slopping a wave over him so that he missed part of it.

". . . and successful. Report next . . ."

Splash.

"Dammit, Phila. Quiet," growled Caesar, shaking water from his face.

"... six hours. Keep schedule."

Caesar snorted. "Keep schedule," he muttered aloud. "We're gonna be shriveled pungets in six hours. Hey, Phila. Have you decided whether we ought to split up here or ..."

Realizing it was very quiet around him, he let his voice trail off. Glancing around, he didn't see her. The water had dropped back to its original level and now lay quiet except for the ripples he caused. Shoving off from the wall, he swam toward the left tunnel, where he'd noticed her last.

"Phila? Hey, toots, you shouldn't go exploring without your Uncle Caesar."

Nothing. Just her torch bobbing on the surface of the water so that the light bounced up and down. Caesar frowned. He felt as though something were blocking his throat so that he couldn't swallow. Two big splashes and nothing. The hair on the back of his neck prickled. He was suddenly aware of his legs dangling down into the water, vulnerable.

"Phila!"

His voice echoed back at him. He grabbed the torch and started swimming as fast as he could. Anything could have grabbed her—tentacles, pincers, anything. She hadn't even been able to cry for help. She was probably fish food by now.

He swam faster, hampered by the gear bag bobbing with him. Maybe it was holding her on the bottom, drowning her. She might still be struggling; she was damned scrappy for her size and fought dirty.

He halted and bit down on his mouthpiece. Bottled air pushed across his tongue and into his lungs. He dove, kicking strongly, and shone the torch toward the bottom of the tunnel. Visibility was about two meters.

And all the time he was thinking he should have felt it pass by, he should have sensed something was wrong when that wave doused him, he should have paid attention to her struggling. If anything happened to her, the boss would never forgive him.

Hell, something had definitely happened to her. Forget thinking "if."

He let himself float back to the surface. There he struck the water with his palm.

"Damn. Phila!" he shouted until his voice reverberated between stone and water. "Phila!"

Ahead, he could see where this branch of the tunnel ended. He frowned, turning around in a circle, and swam back the way he'd come.

Without any warning he felt a sharp tug. For a split second he panicked, certain something finned and nasty had him. He struck out, struggling with all his might, but it sucked him beneath the surface so fast he barely managed to get his mouthpiece back between his teeth.

Only then did he realize that he was caught in a whirlpool, pulling him down to the bottom with such rapidity he couldn't break free. He did his best, but the centrifugal force swept him down. Seconds later he hit the bottom with enough impact to stun him.

And the relentless pull didn't lessen. He scraped through a hole in the bottom of the tunnel, losing his hold on the torch so that he found himself plunged into total darkness. Desperately he reached out, seeking any hold which might give him some purchase. But there was nothing and he kept swirling down like an ant going down a drain, scraped and tumbled until he lost all sense of direction.

I'm okay, he kept telling himself. As long as I have air I'm okay.

He hit bottom again, or maybe it was the side of a wall, and was sucked through another hole. This one was smaller, and he felt himself snag on something sharp. He flung out his hands, but the rip came too quickly to prevent. He lost his mask and airhose all at once. There was no time to catch one last breath. He lost part of his oxygen from his mouth before he clamped lips and nostrils to preserve everything he had left.

And still he was swept on, blind and suffocating. He held his breath until desperation clawed his throat and his lungs began to heave. He held his breath until he felt his heart thudding out of control. He held his breath until his mind went crazy from lack of oxygen. He held his breath until all he knew was a horrible, burning, choking need.

Then his mouth gaped open and he drew in a lungful of

water. His body jerked in shock, but there was no keeping it out. Tumbled helplessly along in that powerful rush, Caesar began to drown.

As the morning sun rose over Byiul, the temperature climbed rapidly until Kelly awakened damp with sweat. He had not slept well. His eyes felt grainy and he rubbed them, yawning, while 41 padded barefoot across the reception room and entered the galley with a bang of the door.

Beaulieu still slept on her pallet, looking more serene and relaxed than she ever did awake. A beam of sunlight found its way through the wooden shutters and glowed upon her dusky skin. Even in the clear light her pointed ears looked natural. The lab had done an excellent job of surgery.

She'd awaken soon. Kelly shoved himself to his feet, feeling stiff from sleeping on the floor all night, and followed 41 into the galley.

Clad only in his linen trousers, 41's muscles rippled beneath his bronzed skin as he stretched, arching his back and going up on his toes. He had Salukan height but human anatomy. Beaulieu grumbled about weird organ placement, but then she grumbled about a lot of things.

Kelly joined 41 in figuring out how to work the processor. Soon, something unrecognizable but smelling hot and delicious ejected on a reflective tray. 41 scooped it off with quick fingers, and Kelly halved it.

"Looks like a meat pie. I thought you wanted cake."

"I only speak Saluk. I can't read it." Closing the processor, 41 took a bite of the pie, which made him yelp. "Good. When it cools."

Blowing on his with more patience, Kelly checked his chron. They had ten hours until Siggerson checked in with the *Valiant*. If he didn't hear from them then, he would wait another two hours. If he still didn't hear from them, his orders were to leave Salukan space as fast as possible.

They'd come in successfully through the planetary defense system yesterday, using the waver shield and praying. Siggerson might make it back in one more time to pick them up.

But if Kelly couldn't get his squad out of the city where they could be teleported . . .

"Kelly," said 41. "Problems?"

Kelly pulled out of his thoughts with a start. "Um? No. Just worrying. Caesar ought to have checked in again. I don't like how far off schedule he's running."

41 snorted. "Everything is off schedule."

"True. Also, our time frame is narrowing. The longer Rafael delays in telling us when we can meet Sparrow—"

Rafael sailed through the galley, startling in an enormous houserobe of fuchsia linen. "Rafael is not delaying anything," he said in irritation, flicking on a fan. "I have to wait until Sparrow contacts me this morning. It will be in the usual drop. Then we will know the rendezvous time and place where you can discuss with him the details of his escape."

Kelly shook his head. "I'd rather have one meet instead of two."

"It's Sparrow who has decided," snapped Rafael. He glared at what they were eating and poured himself a cup of chilled green liquid. "He wants to gather his family. They'll probably be shocked and talk to an official, turning all of us in. I think you should forget the old man and take me instead."

Kelly gazed at him without replying.

Rafael shrugged. "And who is Caesar? Another of your informants here in Byiul?"

"Yes," said Kelly so smoothly 41 gave him a quick glance.

Inside, however, Kelly swore. Rafael was not, absolutely not, supposed to know anything of Caesar's and Phila's existence, much less their end of the mission. Sooner or later the odds were that Rafael would be caught, and Commodore West did not want to lose the snoops installed in the Defended City with him.

Kelly leaned back. "Your network isn't the only one here in Byiul."

That was another lie. Kelly felt Rafael's gaze boring into him and busied himself eating. The pie was too spicy for his taste, but he was too hungry to care.

41, long finished, rose to his feet and glared at Rafael. "How long do we wait for your drop?"

"An hour, perhaps two. I must open for business." Rafael put down his cup and departed hastily.

Kelly and 41 stared at each other.

"Do you trust him?" asked 41.

"Not an inch," said Kelly.

He wandered back to the reception room and set up the portable datatext. Calling up Sparrow's entry, he waited for graphics to compose the man's face.

Extremely narrow—perhaps a scant two centimeters wider than Kelly's hand—with long, sharply etched bone structure beneath weathered skin. The eyes were deep-set but keen, but Kelly saw no arrogance, no war lust, no urge to dominate that was so characteristic of Salukan males. Sparrow had the expression of a scholar: inquisitive, gentle, intelligent. The Empire needed more like him, men and women who were willing to think with their minds instead of with their emotions, who were willing to open themselves to new ideas, to consider ways other than their own, to curtail their urge to conquer and dominate for the sake of peace.

Rafael's boy crept softly into the room, obviously fascinated by them in spite of his wariness. Kelly glanced at him, gave him a brief smile, and returned to his reading. 41—now dressed in his blue *chunta*—sat slumped in a chair, occupying himself by flipping his dagger into the air and catching it, over and over.

Ignored, the boy edged closer, his eyes wide as he watched 41. Kelly glanced at him from the corner of his eye and wondered how old he was. Small and scrawny as though he had never been properly nourished, he scratched the stubble on his shaven head and hunkered down on his bony haunches so that his head did not come much higher than 41's elbow. After a moment 41's lips tugged into a slight smile. Without glancing at his audience he began to flip the dagger more elaborately, catching it sometimes by the hilt, other times by the tip. The boy drew in an audible breath, but 41 smiled at him and showed him his uncut fingers.

The boy studied his hands in visible amazement, then

shrank back in fresh shyness. 41 extended the dagger to him hilt-first. A narrow brown hand, scarred and nicked, reached out and stroked the hilt.

"Hold it," said 41, and pressed the boy's fingers around the hilt.

Entranced now, the boy looked the dagger over, caressing the shining blade, then holding it up to make it flash in the sunlight flooding the room. His mouth stretched with silent laughter as he reflected the light into dancing squares upon the wall.

Beaulieu, fresh-showered and brisk, came from the other end of the apartment. Kelly made a shushing gesture at her and she halted to watch 41's gentle hand signals as he tried to show the boy how to flip the dagger.

She sat down beside Kelly, her expression keen with approval. "Promising," she murmured. "He's shown evidence of loyalty, but any creature will do the same if treated kindly. That he can show kindness in return is something I wasn't certain of."

Kelly frowned. "Of course he can," he retorted with equal softness. "He's not a pet we're trying to domesticate. You sound like one of those idiot psychologists on Station 4."

"Thank you," she said with mock coolness.

Realizing what he'd said, Kelly grimaced in apology.

Beaulieu, however, didn't act offended. "41 isn't an average—"

"Of course he isn't," snapped Kelly. "Neither am I. Neither are you. Average is a statistic. We're all unique."

"I *know* that. But just because you've made an emotional decision to trust him does not mean he has completely adjusted to a normal way of life by the definitions of our culture. He remains unpredictable."

"What is this?" said Kelly angrily. "Are you siding with Rafael?"

She blinked in surprise. "Not at all. I meant he could just as easily have turned on that child."

Kelly frowned. "Why should he?"

She shrugged. "Reminders of his own background and—"

"You're playing head games, Doctor."

"Want to bet?"

Before Kelly could stop her she rose to her feet and walked over to 41 and the boy. At once the boy ducked his head and started to scuttle away, but 41 grabbed his wrist and held him by his chair.

Two faces, one adult and one young, stared up at Beaulieu with a nearly identical lack of expression. Hostile distrust tempered by caution, Kelly realized. He moved to the edge of his chair, ready to stop her if she went too far.

"I'd like to examine your friend, 41," Beaulieu said, smiling at the boy, who shifted his gaze away. "His deafness may be—"

"It was done to him," said 41 harshly. He clamped his free hand on the boy's head and tilted it despite the boy's squirming to show Beaulieu the small puncture scar.

Hearing her angry intake of breath, Kelly rose to his feet. "Is that true?" he demanded.

41's yellow eyes flashed to him, then back to Beaulieu. "Look at his throat. See the scar where they cut his vocal cords?"

"God, those barbarians. Let me get my scanner."

As she turned to pick up her medikit, 41 released the boy, who bolted from the room.

"41! Why did you let him go?"

41 stared at her in anger. "Because we frightened him. He probably thinks we are going to take his eyes next."

She blinked. "Is that done?"

41 snorted, but it was Kelly who answered her.

"Of course it is, Doctor. Salukans, especially the lower classes, believe in strict punishments for disobedience. He probably overheard something he wasn't supposed to or answered back when he was reprimanded."

"That's horrible!" She turned back to 41. "You'll have to lure him back. I can cure him. The simplest operation would do it."

41 went back to flipping his dagger. "He's a slave. Not worth the effort."

Beaulieu's dark eyes flashed. "I see," she said icily. "I never thought you, of all people, would have that attitude."

41's dagger spun end over end and smacked into his palm. He clutched the hilt, his tawny eyes as fiery as hers. "It is the way Salukans think. Do not assume what I think."

"All right," she said. "I won't. Tell me, 41, what you would do with the boy."

Kelly started to stop her, then held back. 41 looked past her at Kelly and scowled.

"I do not like tests," he said. "I am not a subject for your analysis or your curiosity."

Beaulieu looked annoyed. "Stop being so damned touchy. I'm not analyzing you. I'm asking for your recommendation."

Shaking back his long tangle of blond hair, 41 jerked to his feet. Walking over to the window, he stood gazing out with his back to them.

Beaulieu and Kelly exchanged glances. He frowned and shook his head. She'd had her chance. Enough was enough.

Her own expression turned bland. "I'm going to cure that boy," she said. "At least as much as I can."

She started from the room, but 41 whirled from the window.

"No!" he said angrily. "You are a fool to change him. Leave him be."

Beaulieu faced him. "I don't understand. Why should I deny him a chance to—"

"You will kill him."

She stiffened. "The procedure is simple and quite safe. If you have doubts about my skill as a—"

"He is safe as he is now. He has a home and a rich master who can afford to feed him," said 41 harshly. He glared at Beaulieu, unconsciously gouging the windowsill with his dagger point. "If you change him, he will know there are other futures. He will try to run away, and he will be punished—beaten—for it. He will be starved to make him weaker, to keep him the way he is now. Or he will be cut again."

"Nonsense!" said Beaulieu. "Those are ridiculous reasons for denying him treatment. You didn't stay a slave yourself. Why should he have to?"

Color burned beneath 41's cheekbones. He cast Kelly a single, accusing look.

"41," began Kelly, but 41 cut him off.

"Will you take the boy with us?"

Kelly winced. "How do we stop finding another who should go? And another? And another? Once we start letting pity get the better of us, we—"

"See?" said 41 to Beaulieu. "It is the human way to offer selective compassion, handing out gifts and speaking of freedom. But you would do better to kill the boy than to give him a wider comprehension of his misery."

She frowned, the anger fading from her face. "I'm sorry," she said. "I wasn't thinking past my scalpel again. Doctors are trained to have tunnel vision: if something can be treated, do so. I—"

"Stop," said 41. "I've seen you poke Kelly to anger so you can watch him. Why apologize for doing the same to me?" He suddenly gave her a twist of a smile. "Especially when I was doing it to you."

Beaulieu stared. "What? No, you weren't. You . . ."

As she trailed off doubtfully, Kelly laughed. "Hoist with your own petard, Doctor."

She rounded on him. "Did the two of you cook this up?"

Still laughing, Kelly caught 41's eye and winked. "N-no."

41 said, "Do you think me incapable of outmaneuvering you on my own?"

She opened her mouth, then closed it. She looked at them both in suspicion, then pointed at the splinters 41 had made on the windowsill.

"Good try, 41. But I'm not fooled. It wasn't a game with you."

41's smile faded. "That is right," he said angrily. "I am a maladjusted half-breed who looks *promising but unpredictable*."

Beaulieu flinched. "I—"

"I never knew my parents. I was kidnapped from those who raised me. I escaped from slavery, only to be caught by others and sold into hard labor on a colony moon run so strictly we had numbers instead of names to make sure fifty people per support pod came inside to safety every night. When I escaped from that, I found a place with mercenaries who killed for money and betrayed each other for money.

"Adjust, Doctor?" he continued. "I can adjust to anything, anywhere. If I choose to."

"I know," she said calmly. "You've proven that simply by the fact of your survival."

Something flickered in 41's eyes. He put his dagger away. "If you help the boy, he will probably betray us. He knows we do not belong here."

Beaulieu sighed, and Kelly saw her eyes making evaluations. "It's the commander's decision," she said.

Kelly looked at them both and wondered if they had been in secret league on this. He raised his hand in surrender. "One liberated slave coming up."

Beaulieu smiled. "I'll start getting ready."

She hurried into the galley. Kelly cocked his head at 41.

"Well?" he said. "Rafael's not going to like us taking his property."

"Thank you," said 41. "I will get the boy."

He went down the stairs into the stockroom. Kelly shook his head and went into the galley.

"Round one for me," said Beaulieu smugly, laying out the contents of her kit. "Confess, Kelly. You've never gotten him to talk that much about himself before."

"Stop pushing him," said Kelly.

"It's my job," she retorted. "I'll push him just as I push you. This is the most high-pressure job I can imagine. If I don't find the cracks, you or me or Caesar or any of us could fly apart at a crucial moment. Relax, Commander. I know what I'm doing."

"I hope so," said Kelly. "Because if you—"

The sound of running footsteps made him break off. He backed out of the galley just as 41 came bursting through the door.

"Move!" said 41 before Kelly could ask what was wrong. "Troopers closing in for a search. Rafael's holding them at the door."

Kelly swore and glanced over his shoulder at Beaulieu. "Grab your gear. We're leaving."

Without giving her a chance to react, he ran to join 41, who was disconnecting the jammer and cramming it into its pack. Kelly snatched up the datatext and rolled their pallets up to stuff them into the duffles. With her medikit under her arm, Beaulieu rushed through the rest of the apartment for a quick check to erase any traces of their presence. Kelly swung two duffles over his arm, leaving the jammer and weapons case for 41.

Kelly started down the stairs while 41 waited for Beaulieu. Shoving the doctor ahead of him, 41 brought up the rear with his Brud in his hand.

How long could Rafael stall the troopers? Kelly hurried through the clutter of the stockroom to the back exit leading into the narrow alley. In broad daylight they were going to look very suspicious on the street.

"Hsst!"

Kelly glanced back and saw 41 gesturing at the opposite end of the stockroom. Kelly frowned in bewilderment. 41 shoved past Beaulieu and led them to a far corner. Shoving some empty crates out of the way, he knelt over a trapdoor.

Dropping the duffles, Kelly helped him lift it. A metal ladder led down into darkness. Kelly gestured for 41 to go first. Then he lowered the gear to him, glancing often over his shoulder at the door between the stockroom and the shop. He heard angry voices and shoved Beaulieu down the ladder so roughly she nearly slipped. Then he pulled the crates as close as he could. But the shop door opened, and he heard Rafael saying, "This is an outrage. My loyalty has never been—"

Kelly lowered himself swiftly and closed the trap. It was fitted with an electronic lock. Kelly frowned at the keypad with its undecipherable Salukan symbols and glanced down. Below him, 41 had a torch on.

"Hit top left, diagonal down to bottom right, top center," said 41.

Kelly punched buttons rapidly, sweating. With a soft whir, the lock engaged, and he sagged in momentary relief.

But a thorough search would locate this hiding place. He skimmed the rest of the way down the ladder.

"Rafael told you about this place. What else?"

41 pointed. "That way leads out through an abandoned warehouse. We should reach it before the troopers break this lock. Rafael also got the info drop. We're to meet Sparrow at Tupsetshe Park, west entrance, at the twelfth hour."

"High noon," murmured Beaulieu, grabbing one of the duffles.

Kelly hurried down the tunnel, shining his own torch ahead. It was a narrow, dusty place, drifted with insect webs, and smelling of stale air. "How the hell did they find out about us? Maybe this is just some hassling from DUR."

41 snorted. "Our little friend ran straight out of here and grabbed the sleeve of the nearest trooper on street patrol."

Beaulieu looked at him in shock. "No! I can't believe—"

"I warned you, Doctor," said 41 grimly.

"But we meant him no harm. We were going to help him." She hitched the duffle strap higher on her shoulder. "Damn. I suppose he didn't realize that."

"Even a starving dog will bite the hand that offers it food," said 41.

Kelly glanced at her stricken face and asked 41, "Do you think they will beat anything out of Rafael?"

"Unknown. Probably not yet. The boy can't tell them what he knows, so this is probably just a random search. But remember, Kelly. Rafael warned us that DUR was watching him. This may be all they need to eliminate him."

"You mean take him to prison."

41 bared his teeth. "What's the difference?"

6

And the sun-god Ru did take unto him Solan, lovely goddess of the moon, and her handmaidens Rain and Wind. This union filled the skies with radiance, and we served no more Shevul, ruler of the void.

—School Manual,
general mythology

High noon in Byiul. The sun blazed down, its glare bleaching color from the city. The inhabitants had a flat, one-dimensional look to them as they strolled by. The streets were busier than Kelly expected; unlike most hot-climate populations, Salukans did not have the custom of siesta. Covered walkways provided shade for pedestrians. Plentiful fountains splashed, the sound providing an illusion of coolness.

Kelly touched his wristband with a frown, telling himself he had to give up on Caesar and Phila. They had never checked in a second time. That meant they'd been captured or were dead. Either way, he couldn't help them. He had strict orders to concentrate solely on bringing Sparrow out, no matter what it cost. The tactician in Kelly agreed with those orders, but his heart ached with frustration.

He wanted to take the Defended City apart stone by stone, to reduce that infamous complex of palaces fabled to be the most beautiful in the galaxy to a pile of smoking rubble. He wanted to show these arrogant Salukans that they weren't supreme.

The cross streets showed him glimpses of those mighty walls, built on oppression and mortared with blood.

Kelly gave his head a shake. The heat was making him fanciful.

He walked at a steady pace, finding occasional scraps of shade deliciously cool. There he would pause and try to lower his heart rate with a moment of rest. The ends of the headdress wrapped about his face were soaked with sweat. He had to take frequent rests or risk keeling over with heatstroke. Most of the Salukans passing him, however, looked unaffected by the heat. He knew the day's temperature wouldn't reach its maximum for another two hours. By then, he hoped to be done with Sparrow and back indoors.

Just ahead of him loomed the imposing Treasury of Genisset House. All of the five major houses and most of the minor forty had their treasuries located along this avenue. Treasuries were essentially strongholds where the communal wealth of an entire house was guarded, but they served larger functions as well. Advocates, accountants, banking services, birth and marriage records, museum collections, and law enforcement were only some of those functions provided to every nomarch and his household.

Kelly halted near the steps of the equally impressive Treasury of Juvanne House directly across from Genisset. The Treasury of Juvanne flew the Pharaon's flag, and for a moment Kelly was afraid that meant the Pharaon was coming here today. He didn't want to get caught in a parade, with an army of bodyguards on the lookout for anyone even remotely suspicious in appearance. Then he remembered that Nefir V and his dynasty belonged to Juvanne lineage.

Kelly slipped his fingers inside his headdress to wipe some of the perspiration collected there. Get it over with, he told himself, and crossed the street during the first break in traffic.

The Genisset Treasury looked like a temple. It towered upon a tall foundation, with a broad apron of granite steps and ornately carved columns that rose perhaps two stories high. Each column had been carved as a single piece from pale, translucent stone. A mosaic floor led inside through wide, double doors standing open. Only a handful of citizens moved about inside the round foyer that appeared almost large enough for the *Valiant* to land in.

Kelly's footsteps echoed lightly in counterpoint to the soft murmur of voices. Two more columns adorned with fantastic reptilian motifs of wrought metal supported the domed ceiling far, far overhead. The walls of pale yellow marble veined with scarlet glowed as a backdrop to banks of flickering datatext screens. A life-size holo of a woman draped in opulent fabrics shimmered upon the stairs, ready to greet any visitors desiring to enter the museum wing. On the opposite side of the foyer, a pair of guards in traditional Genisset battle dress flanked a door marked NO ENTRY. Over them hovered a security monitor.

Kelly quickly skirted that and approached a thin, elderly man in a wig of thin black plaits and plain, bureaucratic clothing.

The man's dark, observant eyes sized up Kelly and his rumpled, dusty clothes. Yet courteously he inclined his stiff neck and said, "*Hut eth saluent a ta*."

Kelly inclined back and prayed for his best accent. "Greetings and respect to you as well, domei."

The old man brightened slightly. "You have come for Carnival, hillman?"

"Ahe," said Kelly. "Yes, but I have another task beyond that."

Nervously, aware that he had told no one—not West, not anyone in his squad—that he was going to do this, Kelly unrolled a chamois and held out a long dagger with an ornately carved blade and jewel-studded hilt. It was as much a work of art as a weapon. Well-worn and ancient, its beauty still caught at Kelly's heart every time he held it.

The old man drew in his breath appreciatively. "A Genisset ancestral dagger." He started to touch it, then drew back his hand to frown at Kelly. "How do you come by this, hillman? You are not of our house."

"It belongs to the eldest son of the Mailord Duseath ton Genisset g Forault," said Kelly quickly.

The old man hissed, his eyes narrowing. "Duseath is dead?"

"Ahe."

"How? When? His squadron is stationed . . ." The old man caught himself and drew back, looking angry and more suspicious than ever. "How come you by this?"

"I bought it on Thyrlos," said Kelly. "From a *vasweem* trader. I could see it was an ancestral weapon. It should not be in the hands of strangers. Because my mother was Genisset, I have brought it to you in the spirit of Carnival. I know no more about it."

He handed the dagger to the old man and hurried out. Impossible to tell the man that he had captured Duseath on the miserable ice planet Chealda. Impossible to say that he had promised Duseath to send the dagger to Duseath's son. Impossible to say that his love of Salukan weapons had won over his word of honor until this mission came up and his conscience got the better of him. Impossible to say that Duseath had managed to kill himself in an Alliance security facility rather than remain a prisoner.

The old man followed him. "Hillman, wait! Let us thank you properly. Let us give you full hospitality—"

Kelly quickened his stride, the heat blasting him in the face as he went down the steps and joined the pedestrians in the street. He resisted the temptation to glance back. He had done it in full daylight and no one had realized he was a human. That was enough luck for one day.

Now he had just enough time to get to Tupsetshe Park and meet Sparrow.

Twenty minutes later Kelly was hurrying along Stolat Quay toward the arched stone bridge spanning Centime Canal when a hand in the crowd gave him a violent shove that nearly knocked him off his feet. Kelly twisted, frantically trying to catch his balance. A dagger slashed his *chunta*, aiming high at his chest where the cord of his wallet should have been concealed beneath his clothes.

Kelly let himself drop to the ground. The impact upon unyielding stone hurt, and pedestrians around him moved back, offering no help. Fending off a second dagger thrust, Kelly glimpsed his attacker's eyes above a ragged edge of cloth that concealed the rest of his face.

His attacker was nothing more than a common thief bold enough or hungry enough to strike in daylight.

Furious at letting himself be caught this way, Kelly gave a vicious twist to the man's knife wrist and chopped him just below the throat. The thief doubled up, coughing, and Kelly was able to squirm free. He scrambled to his feet and kicked the thief, sending him sprawling.

That should have been the end of it, except the man yelled and came at Kelly a second time. Cursing, Kelly ran for it, dodging through the crowd, which parted in confusion as he shoved.

Not a common thief, Kelly thought angrily. The man had to be a DUR agent in disguise. And he'd blundered right into the trap.

He could lose his pursuer or he could stop and fight him again. Either option called attention to him. The last thing he needed was for a curious trooper to come into this.

And meanwhile, he was fourteen minutes short ofhis rendezvous time with Sparrow and running full speed away from the park.

He ducked off the street into an alley wide enough for two people to walk abreast. Veiled women sat in doorways, clicking castanets in invitation for him to enter. Thin music on a scale irritating to his human ears wailed from an upper balcony. He stumbled and lurched to an abrupt halt, putting a hand on the wall to hold himself up. His heart went at hyperdrive, and he felt as though he were drowning in perspiration. The heat was suffocating. He couldn't keep up this killing pace.

Glancing back, he saw the agent coming. With a groan Kelly pushed himself away from the wall and forced himself to jog on. The agent gained on him. Kelly quickened his speed and kept going until he came to a cross alley. He whipped right and halted there out of sight, sucking in great gulps of air and holding his breath as long as he could in an effort to slow down his panting. He drew his Brud, listening to the agent approach.

But the footsteps slowed and stopped. Kelly swore beneath

his breath. The agent was too wily to be caught by ambush. Fine. Kelly had other tricks.

He slid his shoulder blades along the wall until he reached the corner. Tightening his grip on the Brud, he drew in a breath and gathered himself. As soon as he heard the soft scrape of a wary footstep, he flung himself around the corner and fired.

The range was nearly point-blank. The massive slug hit the Salukan in the chest and sent him flying back. His dagger spun in a graceful arc and landed with a clatter near Kelly's foot.

Crouching, Kelly scooped it up while along the alley women cried out and ran into their houses. Kelly grimaced to himself. Witnesses would have troopers here in a matter of seconds. He had to hurry.

Tucking away his Brud, he searched the agent swiftly, his hands avoiding the massive wound and gush of amber blood soaked into the dirty *chunta*. Nothing. Not even a standard-issue blaster. Damn.

Kelly ripped off the man's headdress and felt along the twisted coils of cloth. His fingers touched something small and hard. Tucking the headdress under his arm, Kelly ducked out of sight in the cross alley and tore the headdress apart.

The transmitter looked like a cheap, carved amulet, but when Kelly pulled it apart the hollowed halves did not contain a snippet of the owner's birthing hair dipped in the blood of his mother but instead a tiny circuit chip. Pocketing it, Kelly jerked off his ripped *chunta* to pull it inside out. The troopers would be looking for a hillman in a red *chunta*. His was now green. Pulling it back on, he belted on his dagger and concealed the agent's weapon up his sleeve. The slash in his *chunta* was a problem. Kelly bent over and cut some more rips in the hem of his *chunta*, then frayed the knee of his trousers.

He walked away quickly, circling back to the crowd at Stolat Quay. A security monitor hovered above the street, and a loudspeaker ordered all citizens to line up along the quay wall. A squad of troopers marched past, their blue-black wigs dusty, the sun glinting on their blasters.

Lined up behind a giant of a woman in a yellow *sulla* which obscured her from head to foot, Kelly pulled the transmitter from his pocket and dropped it into the water. DUR might know that the dead thief in the alley was one of theirs, but then again they might waste some time looking for their agent at the bottom of the canal.

Kelly glanced worriedly at his chron. Two minutes until the rendezvous. He wasn't going to make it. That left everything up to 41, who might also have fallen into a DUR trap.

Who set us up? Kelly asked himself angrily.

It had to be Rafael, who must have talked as soon as Kelly, Beaulieu, and 41 escaped from his shop. Which meant Sparrow had been compromised also. Tupsetshe Park was now no-man's-land.

Kelly's identity papers were superb fakes, but the troopers only needed a good close look at his face to be suspicious. And as soon as they identified the body as a DUR agent, all hell was going to break loose.

Kelly edged closer to the woman in the *sulla*. A kinsman could legally kill him for speaking to her while she was in mourning. But no one seemed to be with her. Since his only other option was jumping into the canal, he decided to risk it.

"Excuse my presumption, dama, but—"

"You look hot, hillman," whispered a husky, feminine voice.

Although Kelly found it disconcerting to speak to a pillar of yellow cloth and wasn't sure if she faced him or had her back to him, he inclined politely.

"The day is not well, dama," he said softly, half of his attention on the loud-voiced minlord coming slowly down the line. "And I have come out without my papers."

"Perhaps," she said, sounding amused. "Or perhaps you are the troublemaker they search for. There is always excitement during Carnival, especially in this district. You came from the Street of Houirs. Are you tired from their pleasures, hillman?"

The open invitation in her voice offered Kelly the chance

he'd been looking for. Putting a smile into his eyes, he said warmly, "Not at all, dama."

She loosed a soft ripple of laughter. "So polite. You amuse me. Stand closer."

Kelly obeyed, wondering what he was getting himself into and not caring as long as he escaped arrest. A slender hand gloved in transparent fabric emerged from a side slit in the *sulla* and clasped his forearm.

"Say nothing," she whispered as the minlord approached them.

Kelly swallowed hard and tried to look like a kinsman.

The minlord had small, porcine eyes and such heavily ridged bone structure he looked prehistoric. Kelly felt cold low in his guts. The woman could just as capriciously decide to turn him in as help him.

"Don't get close to the natives," warned the AIA sociologist in charge of Kelly's culture briefings. "Avoid direct contact with any individual if possible. If you must make contact, do not trust any of them no matter how friendly they may seem. Salukans delight in double-dealing. They are never what they appear to be on the surface."

After an interminable moment the minlord swung his gaze away from Kelly to the woman. *"Hut, dama. Comme qu'sce thet?"* he said politely.

"I think this is a waste of my time," she replied. "What is the crime which has been done, and why should it impede my progress?"

The minlord inclined, obviously comparing the rich yellow cloth she wore against Kelly's tattered, everyday linen. "The murder of a tribesman is nothing which should concern you, dama. I apologize for the inconvenience. Who is this man with you?"

She laughed, and Kelly's muscles tightened. She sounded too relaxed, too amused. She was going to turn him in. He glanced at the canal, ready to jump.

Her fingers tightened on his arm. "Our little mischief maker, a disciple of Than. His *proctur* wishes him to be converted to the order of Askanth, but it is a tedious process.

His education has so many gaps." She sniffed. "These eastern hillmen . . . you know what they are like."

"Ahe." The minlord smiled unpleasantly at Kelly, who forced himself to return his gaze. "Happy schooling."

To Kelly's relief and amazement, the minlord moved on past them with a harsh demand for the next person's papers. Minutes later the crowd was allowed to disperse. Kelly turned to the woman with his thanks, but she did not release his arm.

"Not so much haste, hillman," she murmured. "I have named you as my escort and you will remain so. There are discreet ways to leave my house. And the monitors tracking us will be fooled completely. *Compri?*"

Kelly swallowed hard, glancing across the canal at the park shimmering in the heat. He understood her point, but he had to meet Sparrow. Otherwise, they had risked their lives to get here for nothing.

"Dama," he began. "I—"

She shifted her grip on him and Kelly found himself staring at the needle-sharp tip of a tiny silver stiletto pressed against the inside of his wrist. He tensed.

"I have risked much for your sake," she murmured angrily. "Do not make fools of us both."

She was right. The minlord still watched them from the quay. A security monitor hovered nearby. If Kelly left the woman and entered the park, the monitor would probably follow him. That meant 41 would just have to take care of Sparrow on his own.

Kelly shrugged. "I am honored to be your escort wherever you want to go."

The heat felt good on 41's back as he knelt to take cover within a copse of tall, flowering shrubbery. Sprinklers sprayed a fine mist of water over the park foliage, creating miniature rainbows in the sunlight. 41's damp clothes stuck to his body as he crept closer to the bench. Sparrow sat on it, pretending to eat his lunch. But 41 could see the man's hands shaking, and he scattered more food on the ground for the inquisitive, almost tame ground rodents than he actually ate.

A DUR agent also crouched in the shrubbery, watching Sparrow. 41 had already killed his colleague, slipping up behind him and stabbing him through the ear straight into his brain. Now he stalked the remaining one, aware of the fact that Kelly had not turned up, aware that soon Sparrow would go. 41 ignored the time pressure and concentrated on his quarry.

This agent was more alert. He kept shifting his stance slightly, checking each direction. He held a blaster in his hand.

You are my meat, thought 41, visualizing the kill. The muscles in his back twitched. He crept closer.

When he reached striking range, he paused, settling himself on his haunches and taking out his dagger. A knife throw was risky, but he did not fear risks.

Hefting the dagger in his hand, he judged the agent's next move, waiting until he half turned in 41's direction, then threw. The dagger blade winked silver in the sunlight and thunked deep just below the agent's throat. He fell with a thud onto the soft earth. 41 scrambled to him quickly and confiscated the blaster. Sinking his dagger into the damp mold to clean it, he pushed his way from the shrubbery and sat down beside Sparrow just as the old man started to leave.

"Greetings, domei," he said. "Would you like to buy a dagger? Very good price."

Sparrow looked tired and worried. He shook his head and turned away.

"Sparrow," said 41, making him start. "I'm with Peregrine. You had better sit down and haggle with me. We have much to talk about."

Arnaht stared at him for a long moment, then slowly sank to the bench as though his legs would no longer support him. 41 handed him the dagger, and he took it as though he had never seen one before.

"Quickly, old man," said 41 impatiently. "There are traps everywhere. We have not much time. Are you ready to leave?"

"Yes," said Arnaht. "That is, I have to wait a little longer."

41 frowned in suspicion. Perhaps Sparrow had lost his courage and betrayed them. If so, he would kill Sparrow to avenge Kelly and Caesar and Phila.

"Why?" he asked harshly. "What trick are you playing?"

Arnaht raised agitated hands. "No, no. It is my son. He may betray me. He is ashamed of me. He—"

41 swore and glanced around swiftly. "When did you tell him?"

"Last night."

"There was a trap set here with you as bait. There is no maybe about your son. He has betrayed you. Come!"

"No, wait." Arnaht pulled free of 41's clasp. "My daughter is willing to defect with me, but she lives within the Defended City. She will be able to visit me this afternoon. Then we—"

"She will be watched and followed. So will you." 41 shook his head. He smelled another trap, and he did not like it. "No, you must abandon her. It is too dangerous to wait."

Arnaht lifted his hands to his face and rocked a moment in grief. "She is my child. You ask me to cut out my own heart."

41 glared at him, tempted to walk away and leave the old man to his doom. But the Alliance wanted Sparrow. Kelly wanted Sparrow. 41 fought off exasperation and made one last try.

"Some of us have already died for you," he said angrily. "We must leave Byiul before twilight when the city perimeters are closed."

"Yes, I—"

41 took his dagger and rose to his feet. "We shall meet in four hours in Sang Quarter at the street marked 119r. Can you get there without being followed?"

The old man stood up. Determination overcame the fear in his face. "Yes," he said. "I shall find a way."

41 didn't believe him, but he could do nothing more here. With a nod he walked away.

Humming softly as it floated along, the monitor followed them halfway across the city and into the temple complex.

Alarmed by the monitor's persistence, Kelly had little interest in the spacious, walled compound with several open gates allowing people to come and go at will. Lovely pools and fountains shimmered in the heat. One enormous temple dominated the compound, but there were several small, circular ones as well. Across from them stood a row of multistory buildings like barracks. They were built plain, with small round windows.

Kelly paused at the bottom of the stone steps leading up to a door set in one of the barracks. "I need to come in," he said. "For a while."

She had long since put away her knife. She gathered up the long folds of her *sulla* and started up the steps. "I want you to come," she said. "Follow."

The door looked ancient, but it was fitted with a sophisticated electronic lock. She pushed the keys rapidly and said, "If anyone is inside, do not speak. I do not want the *proctur* to hear of this incident."

"Because you're in mourning?"

As soon as he spoke, Kelly knew he'd made a mistake. She glanced back at him sharply, invisible beneath the cloth. Kelly tensed, mentally reprimanding himself for getting too cocky about his knowledge of their customs. He knew nothing about the priesthood, and his culture briefings had steered clear of it.

"The *prOcturs* do not like security monitors coming into the compound," was all the woman said, however. "This one has unusually strong programming. Come."

She swung open the door and went inside.

Following, Kelly found dry, cool air that smelled of old stone, earth, and exotic spices. The niche in the wall supporting a rounded stone carved within another stone surprised him. He realized he was in her personal quarters, for the *gamatae*—mother stones—were strictly for the home and never for public display.

Kelly swallowed and considered taking his chances outside. In his experience, women invited him home for one reason. It would take one touch for her to discover he was human.

He stepped back. "Dama, perhaps I'd better—"

She gestured quickly for silence. "Wait in the vestibule."

The vestibule was a shadowy place. Kelly glanced around at the sparse furnishings and the carved walls and eased toward the door. But his benefactress reappeared almost at once, dismissing her servants. Kelly started to follow them as they filed out, but a massive bodyguard armed with two charge-swords, a dagger, and a pouch full of small metal balls fitted with spikes moved to block Kelly's path. He closed the door and stood in front of it, looking through Kelly with a gaze as impersonal as obsidian.

Kelly eyed him nervously. "Does he have to stay?" he asked.

She laughed in reply, and Kelly wondered if he'd made another mistake. He touched the Brud in his pocket. He could not afford to blow his cover.

The woman removed her *sulla* and tossed it aside, standing revealed in a flared scarlet jerkin and wide trousers of transparent gauze. She topped Kelly by at least a foot, and her bare arms were muscular, almost brawny. Serpentine *fraileths* wrought of gold encircled her biceps. She wore her hair cropped very short in front of her ears and across the top of her skull, then falling in a straight shining mass of black to her shoulders. A wide, heavy collar studded with rubies adorned her throat. The jewels winked as she drew breath.

Kelly stared and she smiled, baring her teeth all the way back to her small fangs, which had been painted scarlet.

"I am a priestess of Askanth, huntress and symbol of kindness to strangers."

She was both fascinating and scary. Kelly found himself unable to look away.

She laughed. "Bare your face, Earther. I would look upon my quarry."

Alarms went off inside him. He turned to run for it, but the bodyguard still blocked the door, impassive and immovable. Kelly reached for his Brud.

"Draw no weapons!" she said sharply. "Hrlar would have to kill you, and that would be a pity. You have sanctuary here within the temple complex. It is a tradition. Any stranger invoking Askanth's name must be given water and shelter for the night."

Kelly moistened his dry mouth and said the first inane comment that occurred to him: "It's not night."

"Not yet." She beckoned. "Come, Earther. Put away your fear. You wanted my help and I gave it to you. Now I would seek your conversation. I have never entertained an Earther before. You fascinate me."

She came closer, almost hissing some of her words. The intensity of her gaze seemed to pin him in place. He did not trust her, but at the same time he saw no reason to shoot his way out.

Her apartment windows were small, narrow openings set high near the ceiling. The dim, cloistered air smelled of a perfume cone burning in one corner. He found it hard to breathe. Slowly he relaxed, letting his fingers uncurl from the weapon in his pocket.

At least she wasn't after sex, he thought. Salukans had a strong abhorrence of his kind.

Usually.

"Bare your face for Daria," she said.

Hesitantly he took off his headdress, not certain what to expect. She stared at him a moment, her eyes glowing, then she laughed and surged up next to him.

"Charming! The paint is well done. Tell me," she said, unsheathing a tiny, gilded claw and raking it lightly along his jawline so that he shivered. "Are you dyed this color all over?"

She was alien, bizarre. Her proximity, combined with the perfume and the shadows, made him dizzy. He told himself this was crazy, but as her intense eyes bored into his he felt his mind going numb. His heartbeat kicked up, but somehow he managed to lift one hand and grasp her forearm. He pulled her hand away from his face, blinking hard in an effort to clear his head.

"I thought," he said, struggling for words, "that your kind considers . . . er . . . relationships with my kind a taboo."

She laughed loudly, her voice ringing inside his head. Was the perfume a drug? he wondered. He tried to step away from her, but her arm clamped him close. He could not budge her strength, and her body felt rock solid. She could probably break him in half if she wanted. He did not like feeling helpless.

"Taboos are for the masses," she said. "I can read your thoughts, little Earther. You are not used to being the quarry. For you, it has always been the chase. *Suh*! A new experience. Don't struggle, my shy one. I have mesmerized you with my mind, for I have blood-call and do not care even if your teeth are blunt and cannot bite."

Kelly tried to reach his Brud, but his hands had lost coordination. She grasped his arm and pulled him deeper into the shadows of her room, drawing him into her lair, and he could do nothing to fight the strange lassitude in his limbs. 41 had said blood-call was a myth; apparently it wasn't.

She pressed her palm against his face. He inhaled a sharp, herbal scent that seemed to explode his skull. And he found himself frozen there, unable to move at all while she took a dagger and cut his *chunta* from neck to hem. She pulled it from his shoulders.

"Fascinating," she said, running her hands across his muscular chest. "Very different from us. The smell of your skin is . . ." She sniffed his shoulders and throat.

The drug began to wear off. Kelly blinked and realized he could move. He told his feet to take him out of there, but instead his fingers lifted and touched her cheek as though her will still directed his body. The texture of her skin felt like worn leather, very soft yet resilient.

She tossed her dagger onto the bed and smiled at his puzzlement.

"That is for later," she explained. "In case of vein-burn when madness strikes and it is to the death to separate."

Kelly frowned. Indirect light slanted over her from the high windows, putting her face into shadows and highlights. Her eyes burned with a madness that worried him. Somehow, he had to gain himself time until his head cleared.

"Daria." His throat was so dry it hurt. "Explain vein-burn."

She laughed, the sound booming through him, and padded

away into the shadows. Kelly strained to move his feet until sweat broke out across him, but he could barely shuffle. She returned and held out a soft globe fitted with a sip-straw.

Kelly scowled at her, determined not to drink any of her potions. She looked displeased and put the straw against his lips.

"Drink," she commanded.

His mind felt scrunched. Panicked, he wondered why no one had ever mentioned that some Salukans were telepathic. He tried his best to resist, but in the end his lips parted and she squeezed the liquid into his mouth.

The drink was so spicy it nearly scalded the hide off his throat. While he gasped, trying to get his breath back, she took off her jerkin and began a peculiar, silent dance around him, almost as though she were stalking him. There was a strange buzzing in his head from the potent drink. He felt a stirring in his loins and was furious. He'd be damned if he'd couple with this alien giantess, no matter how many tricks she pulled.

"Good, Earther," she purred, circling him yet again. "You please me already. Perhaps you will be strong enough to live—"

He summoned all his strength and will and pushed himself to one side, but with a harsh cry deep in her throat she knocked him to the floor and fell upon him, sinking her teeth into his shoulder. He felt a sharp sting from the puncture and a hot little trickle of pain, but it was as though the histamines on her tongue jolted straight into his bloodstream, bringing madness with it. He rolled, but she was biting him hard enough to draw blood each time and clawing him. The still-sane corner of his mind screamed for him to get out of this, but the rest of him was lost in the drug fog. His *chunta* with the gun in its pocket lay on the floor where Daria had dropped it, nearby yet far from his reach.

From nowhere she produced a small, silver stiletto and slashed it down his arm. Pain followed like a hot brand.

Daria sucked at his blood. "You taste sweet," she moaned. "I must have it all."

He tried to twist away from her, but his head was roaring

and his limbs remained leaden and clumsy. He wanted to shout aloud in frustration.

She cut her palm and shoved it against his mouth. "Drink of me, little one."

The amber blood welling up along the cut smelled sour, alien. Sickened, he averted his face.

"You deny me!" she shrieked in anger, and struck again with the stiletto, slashing it across his abdomen.

Air hit the wound with a burst of agony that cleared his head. He jerked away from her and flung up his arm to block another knife slash.

"Damn you!" he shouted. "Get away from me!"

She loomed over him, naked and bloodstained, her eyes savage with madness.

"There is no stopping." She grabbed him by the throat. "I want you, Earther."

The pressure of her fingers upon his windpipe both terrified and infuriated him. Half expecting her to sink her fangs in his carotid, he tore at her hand, prying her fingers loose. She knelt over him, crooning *"C'ai sale, c'ai sale"* over and over again with her eyes half shut.

Come to me.

The hell I will, thought Kelly. From the corner of his eye he saw her raise the stiletto again. With a shout he curled his legs and kicked her hard in the stomach, jarring his heels against her tough abdomen plate.

With a grunt of expelled air she staggered back from him, momentarily stunned, then she bared her teeth. "Better," she said. "Now you understand how it is for us. Again, Earther."

Kelly glanced desperately at the door. Hrlar still stood guard, unmoving and perhaps even bored as though this sort of thing were normal.

Not for me, thought Kelly.

Staggering to his feet, he started for the door, but she ran around him and blocked his way. Kelly shook off a wave of dizziness. His blood flowed out of him, sheathing his stomach. Kelly pressed his hand to the cut. It was deep and long. He'd rather be shot any day than be cut. It hurt damned bad.

He managed to take a few steps, then a wave of dizziness swept over him. With a faint groan he sank to his knees.

At once she pounced, sending him toppling back. He blacked out for a moment, and when he came to he found himself sprawled upon her bed with her crouched beside him. Her eyes glowed expectantly. The dagger lay between them.

His fingers reached weakly for it. With a laugh she snatched it away and nicked his forearm playfully.

"We are ready now," she said, sending prickles of alarm through him. "Ready for union, ready for vein-burn. My little *Earther* . . ."

Growling, she sprang. Kelly rolled at the last minute, scrambling off the bed. He hit the floor broadside. Pain lanced through his ribs, and he pressed his sweating face against the floor, waiting for the spasm to ease up.

Daria got him by the ankle and dragged him away from his clothes, away from the Brud.

Desperately he kicked free of her hand and crawled across the floor.

She jumped off the bed with a thud that jolted him. No longer looking amused, she kicked his clothes farther away.

"If you try to leave, coward, Hrlar will kill you," she said. "I am Daria ten Forault g Maus, high priestess of Askanth. It is an honor to be chosen by me!"

At least she was finally talking again. He gasped for breath, hoping that full rationality would return to her. "Hrlar can do what he likes. I am leaving."

"No!" she screamed. "Leave me in vein-burn? You insult me. I will kill you!"

He struggled to his feet, wondering what she had been doing up till now if not attempting it.

"Crei ta murthe!" she screamed. Lifting the dagger, she came at him.

His depth perception seemed to be going. One moment she looked far away, the next she was on top of him, striking hard with the dagger. He threw up his arm to block the blow and punched her hard beneath the throat with his other fist. She crumpled to the floor, her sides heaving with distress.

Silence spread through the apartment.

Kelly frowned and touched her shoulder. She'd be sore and mad when she woke up, but at least he'd be alive.

Stupid, stupid, stupid to get mixed up in something like this. He should have known better, but self-recrimination could come later. Right now he had to get out of here.

He wiped his face with a shaking hand and tried to collect enough strength to gather his clothes. From the vestibule came a tentative query:

''Dama?''

Stifling a groan, Kelly desperately jerked on his clothes. They stuck to the blood, and he felt sick and clammy. Mustn't get light-headed. Not yet. He gripped his Brud and sought for an explanation as the guard walked in.

''Dama?''

''It's all right,'' Kelly said quickly. ''She's not dead. Just unconscious.''

The bodyguard snarled an oath and charged forward. Kelly braced himself, his pistol ready. Even so, one sword crackling green with lethal runners of energy flashed past his head, missing only because Kelly threw himself flat. He rolled, squeezing off two quick shots, and heard Hrlar grunt in pain. The man fell with enough force to jar the floor.

Panting, Kelly started to lift himself only to duck again, his heart in his mouth, as a spiked ball whizzed past him. It chunked into a nearby wooden chair, sending splinters flying. Kelly fired again, seeing Hrlar's massive body jerk at the impact, then lie still.

Cautiously Kelly waited a moment, the Brud held aimed in both hands. But Hrlar lay as motionless as his mistress. Slowly Kelly let out his breath. His heart thundered, and he felt woozy and weak. He crawled over to Hrlar and checked him, but the man was dead.

Three slugs, when the Infiltration Lab had assured Kelly the slugs were one-shot stops.

The wet stench of blood filled the air. Nausea hit Kelly and he retched until he thought he would pass out. At last he was able to rock back on his heels and catch his breath. His left arm had started bleeding again. He couldn't afford to lose more. Closing his eyes against a series of chills, he tore a strip of cloth off the bed hangings and bound first his waist, then his arm, gritting his teeth as he tightened the knot. That helped, but he wasn't sure he could get out of here in one piece. Even if he managed it, he couldn't go out on the streets dripping red blood.

Wiping his face, he forced himself to think. In the vestibule the yellow *sulla* still lay where Daria had tossed it down. Kelly forced himself to his feet. He put on the garment, nearly throwing up again because it smelled of her.

Don't pass out, he told himself sternly. Walk a straight line.

The room smelled like a charnel house. Guilt burned inside him.

Across the room, Daria moaned and stirred.

Ashamed and sick, Kelly straightened the folds of the *sulla* about him and staggered out.

7

Strategy should be circles within circles.
—maxim of Mailord General Viir

In the administration wing of Godinye Prison, Mailord Cocipec stared at the thin, nervous boy seated across his desk. Around them, screens mounted in the walls flickered constantly with changing scenes from the city as security monitors hovered and followed, scanning the population with constant vigilance. Outside the window, silver flashed in the sun as the wing of a land-shuttle took off from the pad on Godinye's roof and banked sharply to avoid flying over the Defended City.

"Cadet Dausal," said Cocipec, "compose yourself. My aide said you have an accusation against a burean. You have spent all day trying to see me personally. Now you are here. I am delighted to talk with you. Have something to drink."

The boy's black eyes were like burning coals in a face handsomely ridged. He looked at the tray of decanters on the corner of Cocipec's desk, and jerked his hand in refusal.

"I . . . am . . . not . . . thirsty," he said, forcing each word.

Cocipec sighed. Dausal's credentials had been checked before his admittance. His corps commander considered him promising officer material. He had no violations upon his record except for a few youthful misdemeanors which to Cocipec indicated that he was healthy. And his father was a burean well respected in government circles, known for many years of loyal service.

However, this sort of thing was tedious, especially now when the most important investigation of Cocipec's career was going wrong.

No Earthers had been found in Byiul. DUR surveillance of Rafael had failed to find any wrongdoing. A report of three strangers staying in the fat shopkeeper's apartment turned out to be faulty. Investigators found no trace, and although Cocipec wanted to order an intensive search of the premises—including laser scans, microscopic analysis, and a close study of skin oils extracted from wooden surfaces—he could not do so without the proper warrants. The original informant was a half-witted slave belonging to Rafael. He could not be found either. Probably he had invented everything to get revenge on his master for too many beatings. It happened all the time in Byiul.

"Well, speak up," Cocipec snapped, dropping his courteous manners.

Dausal jumped. "I came to make an accusation."

"So you've said. Against a burean. Who?"

Dausal hesitated, his eyes darting about the office.

Cocipec's gaze narrowed in anger. "It is a felony to mock the processes of law. You do so by wasting my time. Either you have an accusation to make or you do not."

Dausal rose to his feet and stood with his face averted. "Mailord, I ask your pardon. It's just that I don't know what to do. My duty compels me to speak out, but my heart is weak." He groaned. "I shame myself."

Cocipec snorted and picked up the comm handset. He had a meeting with the Pharaon in less than an hour and no time for a boy's hysterics. "Krilit, clear this boy from my office."

"Wait, please!" said Dausal desperately. "It's my father. I don't want to turn him in, but he . . . he is a traitor."

The door opened. Cocipec flung up a hand, and the sentries retreated in silence.

"Your father's name," he said sternly, although he already knew. Still, it had to be said and recorded officially or the accusation was invalid.

Dausal's face turned a sickly shade of yellow. "Arnaht," he whispered. "My father's name is Arnaht ton Koult g Von. He is a burean in the Ministry of Information."

Cocipec's heart thudded in interest. "What is his crime?"

Dausal's mouth worked, but it was a moment before he could speak. "T-treachery. Selling information to . . ."

His last word was inaudible. Cocipec asked him to repeat it.

"Earthers!" shouted Dausal. "Stinking darshon Earthers!"

Sinking into his chair, Dausal buried his face in his hands and began to grieve.

Cocipec stared at him for a few seconds, his mind flashing at top speed. Arnaht was a burean of senior lateral rank. That meant he had no official power and no prestigious position, no special transportation privileges, no unrecorded supplements to his salary, and no audience with the Pharaon, but he had access to every file within the Ministry of Information. Through some of those files he had access to other ministries as well. He could do a great deal of damage if he chose.

A chill ran through Cocipec. He started to order an immediate arrest, then curbed himself. Careful, he thought. He must make sure it was true. Dausal could be in error. Cocipec had not achieved the power he now enjoyed by making rash mistakes.

Rising to his feet, Cocipec patted Dausal on the shoulder. "Collect yourself. I'll instruct my aides to hold my calls."

Dausal lifted his head and stared bleakly into the distance as though he had not heard. He looked devastated, older than his years. At any moment he might change his mind and refuse to speak. Cocipec intended to take no chances on regret.

Stepping outside his office, he snapped his fingers.

Krilit came running. "Yes, Mailord?"

"I want a glass of chilled mabry wine prepared with a light dosage of bematheydrol. Just enough to loosen my visitor's tongue, but not enough so that he knows he's been drugged. Tune a listener into my office. Override the screening waves. I want every word he utters recorded. I also want a truth scanner. If he's lying, he goes straight to the mind sieve. Have the interrogation lab standing by."

Krilit's eyes widened. "Yes, Mailord."

"Inform Surveillance to prepare a detail. This will be their last chance to redeem themselves after today's dismal failures. Have them stand by for their instructions."

"Do you want security monitors backing them up?"

"Probably. I may want—"

"Mailord!"

Cocipec turned in annoyance at the interruption and saw Specialist Firult striding up the corridor.

Without acknowledging the specialist, Cocipec snapped his fingers at Krilit. "That is all for now. Get that drink prepared. Move!"

"Yes, Mailord."

Krilit scuttled away, and Firult came to a halt with a smart salute.

Cocipec frowned. "You are off station, Specialist," he said coldly.

Firult, a veteran compaigner with a face drawn and twisted by scar tissue from many old wounds, looked unperturbed. "I have a special report to make. May we go into your office?"

"No."

Firult blinked and glanced around at the three desks supporting assistants, who were goggling at every word. "Mailord, this is not—"

"The time is not convenient," snapped Cocipec, aware of how little time remained before he had to go before the Pharaon with his own special report on his failure to locate the Earther assassins. A dismal report of error, failure, and miscalculation. He hated looking incompetent. "Your report will have to wait, Firult."

Krilit hurried past, carefully carrying a glass filled with blue mabry wine. Cocipec started after him, but Firult moved to block Cocipec's path.

"Forgive me, Mailord. But the deaths in Tupsetshe Park—"

"Silence!"

Firult inclined and stepped back.

Cocipec regained mastery of his temper and gestured curtly. "Come with me."

He led Firult down the corridor and into a small interrogation room for an illusion of privacy. Only Cocipec's office was really secure from snoops.

"Speak quickly," said Cocipec.

Firult coughed. "At the same time our agent was killed in the Street of Houirs near Stolat Quay, two others died in the park. They were dressed in civilian clothes and wore fake DUR transmitters. They carried DUR-issue blasters and standard daggers. But they were military."

Cocipec blinked. "So, so," he said softly, very interested. "Go on."

"Knife work, both times. One was stabbed in the ear. The other below the throat." Firult handed Cocipec a diagram. "This is the preliminary scan of the wounds from the morgue report. See the analysis of the edges? Now compare it with this trace reaction of the flesh against the metal."

Cocipec studied the data carefully, growing more and more excited. "I see. Yes!"

"Shakir-processed steel is the best. We import it on a massive scale. But this has more iron in the alloy—"

"Yes, yes, I see. I understand," said Cocipec impatiently. "The weapon used was of Boxcan manufacture. An Alliance weapon."

"You've wanted proof that Earthers are in Byiul," said Firult triumphantly. "Now you have it. Slim, yes, but we will gather more."

Cocipec glanced up from the diagrams. "Where are the bodies?"

"Still in our morgue. After all, they're disguised as our agents. We have the right to them."

"Keep them." Cocipec paced about the small room, thoughtfully thumping his abdomenal plate. "What in Ru's name is the military up to?"

"Unknown. They were on surveillance detail. We are trying to find out who passed through the park during that time span.'' Firult sighed. ''Not an easy task.''

''No, impossible,'' agreed Cocipec. ''What about our agent? How was he killed?''

Firult bared his teeth. ''Shot, close range. The slug hit his spine and shattered. It will take time to analyze the pieces.''

Cocipec swore. ''Different method. Is there a connection?''

''Unknown. They happened at approximately the same time. Our agent made no report prior to action, but obviously he spotted something suspicious and followed it into the Street of Houirs. The troopers bungled everything, of course. No citizens they've questioned saw anything. And identity papers are very up to date for Carnival.''

Cocipec thought it over. ''I want to know why military is impersonating DUR. It will be a good question to present to the Pharaon shortly. Thank you, Firult. You have done well.''

''Not well enough. I want those Earthers. They laugh at us.''

''Get some rest, but stay within call.'' Cocipec clapped him on the shoulder. ''I may have more work for you.''

He walked out in time to see Dausal, glazed and unsteady, walking down the corridor with an escort. An interrogator stood in the doorway of Cocipec's office, beckoning.

Angry at having missed everything, Cocipec stalked to his own desk and sat down. ''Well?'' he demanded. ''Are you finished already?''

''Yes, the boy spoke readily. Arnaht called his son and daughter to dinner last night and told them he has been selling information to the Alliance for the past seventeen years—''

Cocipec struck his desk. ''Shevul, take my soul!''

''—and that he plans to defect. He urged both Dausal and Melaethia to go with him so that they would not have to face reprisals. The boy has done his duty and should not be—''

''Subjective commentary is not required,'' said Cocipec with a scowl. He sat there a moment, feeling the urge to go out and shoot the nearest pedestrian. Now it all began to fit. The crash of the observer Sharpskeet aircraft on the outskirts of the city, the strangers supposedly staying with Rafael, who was already under suspicion, a ministry burean planning to defect.

The Earthers had not come to assassinate the Pharaon. They had come to collect Arnaht. That filthy, despicable traitor.

Cocipec stood up. "Detain the boy."

"But—"

"I want him in a secure location," snapped Cocipec. "Where is the girl?"

"She is a concubine in the Third Court of Women. So far as we know, she is within the Defended City."

Cocipec frowned. Both of his own daughters had been passed over as concubine candidates. That meant he had to find dowries for them on his salary in addition to paying for military training for one son and scientific training for the other.

But he forced himself to gesture approval. "Good. She can't leave there now. If the old fool was willing to risk discovery by confiding in his children, he may be reluctant to defect without them."

"Perhaps," said the interrogator. "But the fact remains that he has put his family at risk. His behavior cannot be predicted—"

A knock sounded on the door. Krilit looked in without permission.

"Forgive my interruption, Mailord," he said. "But it is time you departed for the Defended City."

"Thank you." Cocipec sighed and gestured dismissal for the interrogator. The Pharaon was not going to like what he had to report. Byiul was supposed to be impregnable. But Cocipec vowed the Earthers and Arnaht were not going to find Byiul as easy to leave as to enter.

He glanced at Krilit. "Have Rafael arrested and his shop closed. Do not wait for warrants. Seize him now."

"Yes, Mailord. Upon your authority."

Within Arnaht's office in the Ministry of Information, Cocipec's gaunt face faded from the screen as he left the range of the snoop. Arnaht released a sigh and sat back, taking care to hide his shaking hands in his lap. Dausal's betrayal—although expected, even counted upon—grieved him.

"There," he said as soon as he could control his voice. "Everything is in place."

"Yes," said Vaudan Raumses' bored drawl. "The pieces of the game are fitting together nicely. You have done well, old man, to amuse me. All we lack are the Earthers—"

"They will be at the meeting point," said Arnaht quickly, too quickly.

He glanced at the vaudan's face and saw displeasure at his interruption. Arnaht rose to his feet, feeling as though he could not breathe. He inclined and held his tongue, knowing better than to babble an apology. Still, he had had to take the chance and mention the Earthers. If the vaudan showed no interest in them, there might yet be a chance to survive this intrigue.

The vaudan, second in power only to the Pharaon himself, towered over the room. Resplendent in a brilliant turquoise and magenta tunic worn over white linen trousers, he looked as fit and muscular as any warrior in the field. His bronze skin gleamed with oils. His narrow face, with the features etched as sharply as wind could cut sand, needed no paint to emphasize his good bloodlines. He wore no wig, and his shaven head reflected the office light. His eyes were small, flat, and petty. Renowned for his bad temper and quick to take offense, the vaudan had fought over two hundred duels before coming to his present position as the Right Hand of Pharaon. Now no one dared challenge him, and he simply had to order the execution of those who displeased him.

He and Nefir had grown up together. They were cousins through the house of their mothers. It was rumored that Raumses wanted the throne for himself, but Nefir would hear no accusations against him and nothing had been proven.

I know the truth, thought Arnaht resentfully. But he dared not use it. His own life hung by too precarious a thread.

"I wonder," said Raumses thoughtfully, walking about the small, shabby office with its sophisticated filing equipment. "I wonder if you are trying to be clever, old man. Are you?"

Arnaht's heart seemed too big for the walls of his abdomen. He lifted his gaze to the vaudan's and said nothing, for no words would be the correct answer.

After a moment the vaudan smirked. "How you quake and shiver. Just remember that I caught you at your game of selling secrets. I have been telling you what to tell the Alliance for the past two years. And bringing them here was my idea. Remember that, if you are tempted to throw the game, old man. I cannot be fooled."

"No, domei vaudan," whispered Arnaht.

Inside, his throat was so full of words he could barely choke them back. Always he had wanted to defect. Always he had resented being Raumses' puppet. Whenever possible, he had changed Raumses' messages to accurate ones. He had not told Raumses the correct rendezvous point for tonight. He wanted to get out. He wanted his freedom.

"As for your precious Earthers," said Raumses, making Arnaht tense, "I am not amused by the deaths of your guardians. And Cocipec's impounding of the corpses is a mistake he will regret. Plus, you have not found the Earthers' hiding place. You are slack, old man. You are careless."

Arnaht felt hollow and incontinent with fear. But more than that, he felt his hatred of this man like a living, pulsing serpent in his belly, eating him alive from the inside out. And he was terrified that it would show.

"I shall try again to contact them, domei vaudan," he said. "They were all at the man Rafael's apartment. Because of Cocipec, they have scattered. I—"

Raumses turned away. "This bores me. Make sure you lead the Earthers straight into my trap tonight."

"I shall not fail."

Raumses' gaze pinned him. "No," he said softly, making Arnaht shiver, "you will not. After all, there is your lovely daughter to consider. I am sure Nefir would be most interested to learn that the father of his newest blossom is a traitor of many crimes."

For a moment the office darkened around Arnaht. He ceased to breathe and there was such pain inside him he thought his last moment had come.

"She is not . . . she remains within the Third Court . . . she has not yet—"

"No?" Raumses laughed. "Your gossip is out of date, old man. She pleases Nefir greatly. I hear they have not left the royal bedchamber for this entire day."

Panic and rage came over Arnaht. He stepped forward, lifting his fists. "You did this!" he cried, his voice breaking. "You brought her to his notice—"

"Unfortunately no. Matchmaking is a woman's game. But I must confess this one is deliciously ironic. She, at least, is safe . . . until the Pharaon tires of her." Raumses bared his small, pointed teeth. "Politics of the inner seraglio. Dangerous predators, the females. She has captured too much favor too soon, and that will mean poison in her cup from the hand of a jealous ex-favorite."

"My child," whispered Arnaht, stricken.

"Yes, you should be proud of her. Not every concubine has had the honor of taking Nefir all the way to vein-burn. He is notoriously hard to please."

Raumses walked to the door where his boydguards waited as impassively as deaf-mutes. "Tonight, old man. Remember where your allegiance lies."

As soon as he was gone, Arnaht sank into his chair and pounded his fists upon his knees. Not Melaethia, not his child. To lose Dausal was bad enough, but he had always known the boy would never accept his personal philosophy of making peace with the Earthers. But Melaethia had an open mind, a willingness to learn and inquire.

It could not be true. He rubbed his face, fighting back the numbness of grief. He must not believe it. She was not finished with her training yet. Nefir would not want her yet. It had to be a lie from Raumses just to keep him in line.

Arnaht's determination returned. He would outwit that posturing, power-hungry gled. By now, Melaethia should be waiting at his apartment. He'd better go home and start preparations for their journey.

But an hour later, when Arnaht reached his building and took the lift up to the fourth floor, he found a light blinking upon his message receiver and an imperial seal emblazoned upon his door. His throat felt constricted, and for a long moment he stood there unable to move.

The imperial seal—a mark of auspicious honor to himself and his family and his house. It meant the Pharaon was thanking him publicly for the gift of his daughter. It meant he would never see Melaethia's face again, never hear her voice again. She belonged to Nefir now, and her beauty could not be shared.

He unlocked the door and walked in like a dead man, his dreams shattered. For him, the game was over.

8

Strike swiftly. It is shameful to lose thy dagger in battle.
—maxim of Mailord General Viir

"We can't stay here," said 41, walking into the warehouse. "We have been betrayed."

Beaulieu rose to her feet and stared at him. 41 took off his headdress and let his sweat-soaked hair tumble to his shoulders. One glance around the empty warehouse told him Kelly was not here. Disappointment filled his chest, and for a moment he was conscious only of a furious urge to attack something.

"Where's Kelly?" said Beaulieu, looking past him. "Is he waiting with Sparrow for us to join him with the gear?"

Weariness weighed down upon 41. If he told her the truth, she would not want to leave. He understood Kelly's orders to salvage the squad if anything went wrong. Well, everything had gone wrong, and all that remained of the squad was him and Beaulieu. His eyes were burning. He could not look at her.

"Yes. We must go now to the perimeter," he said.

She said nothing. After a moment he lifted his head and looked at her. She was frowning.

"You're a damned poor liar, 41."

It was a statement of fact, not an insult. He looked at her, saying nothing.

"What happened? Come *on*, I'm not some quivering female who can't take the truth. Was he killed?"

"Unknown. There was a trap set for us in the park. I dealt with it. But Kelly never came."

She sucked her bottom lip over her teeth in the way she had whenever she was thinking. 41 watched her, waiting for her to accuse him of betraying Kelly. If she did, he would kill her. But she did not and some of the tension left him.

41 frowned, wondering if they should go elsewhere than back to Station 4. He could take the *Valiant* from Siggerson once they teleported aboard and fly it to a refuge in the independent Zeta System.

"The Commodore West," 41 said carefully, wanting her to understand he was being practical, not a coward. "How does he punish failure?"

"What? Who cares about West?" said Beaulieu impatiently. "We've got to find out what's happened to Kelly. How did the two of you get separated?"

"This is wasting time. I could have been followed here—"

Beaulieu gripped his arm. "Tell me."

41 pulled free. "Kelly and I split up. He wanted to visit the Genisset Treasury—"

"Why?"

41 glared at her.

"All right. Never mind why. He went to the Treasury. Go on, then."

"Then nothing. I went to the park and killed the two spies watching Sparrow—"

Beaulieu blinked. "You saw Sparrow? You made contact with him?"

"Why," said 41 impatiently, "do you interrupt?"

"Because you're so slow. If I didn't have to drag every word from you, it would help. Go on."

"Kelly never came. Something happened across the canal. The troopers came and questioned people on the quay. I left by a different route and was not caught in that net. Kelly may have been.'' 41 paused a moment. ''I thought he might come here. But he has not, so he is dead.''

''Not necessarily. He could just be a prisoner.''

41 sighed. ''The difference is small.''

''But it's still a difference.'' Beaulieu walked in a small circle, snapping her fingers. ''We have to find him, get him free.''

''How?'' said 41. ''We cannot break into Godinye.''

Her expression flattened and a look entered her eyes that 41 turned away from. Grief was a private thing. 41 had learned early in his life to make no friends, but he liked Kelly. He did not think he would stay in the Hawks if someone besides Kelly gave him orders.

''What if he's not in the Godinye?'' asked Beaulieu gruffly. ''What if he avoided the trap just as you did? He could be coming back—''

41 picked up part of their gear. ''No. Not now. It's been too long.''

''Then maybe he headed straight for the rendezvous point at the perimeter.''

''Doctor,'' said 41 in annoyance, ''you're inventing hope.''

''And you're asking me to believe that Kelly, Caesar, and Phila are all dead!'' she shot back. ''What if they aren't? We don't have proof for any of them. I think we ought to chance using the comms. The authorities know we're here already.''

41 hesitated, then said, ''I have tried it. Kelly did not answer.''

''Oh.''

He handed her a duffle and she took it automatically without even glancing at him. 41 wondered what was in her that made her deny death so vehemently.

''We must go,'' he said, more gently this time.

She made a visible effort to pull herself together and nodded. ''Right. Where do we meet Sparrow?''

''We don't,'' said 41 grimly.

''Why not?''

''He betrayed us. Or his son did. The old man is frightened. He is being followed and watched. I think he is lying in what he said to me. I told him the time and place, but we aren't going to be there for that trap."

Beaulieu stared at him, her dark eyes hostile. "You mean you're going to betray him in turn and leave him behind?"

41 slung a duffle strap over his shoulder. "Yes. Now, come. If Sparrow has been made to talk, then Rafael will soon be arrested. He knows where we are, and he will tell the troopers. We must leave, get out of Byiul now."

She backed up out of reach. "No."

Anger flashed from him. "You have no choice!"

"Yes, I do. I can't just make a run for it, dammit. That means we've failed, that we came here and busted our guts for nothing. If nothing else, we've got to take Sparrow. We've got to make their sacrifice mean something."

Her voice had turned rough with tears. 41 saw the moisture sparkling in her eyes, but she did not let the tears fall. Her pleading touched him, although he did not let himself be ruled by sentiment.

"You are right," he said at last. "If we bring back Sparrow, it is a way to return to headquarters without punishment."

She looked at him oddly. "That's not what I meant. We won't be punished by AIA if we fail."

41 knew she was lying. She could not care so deeply about making the mission succeed if punishments were not very, very harsh. Yes, it made sense to take Sparrow to West. 41 did not really want to steal an Alliance vessel and hide as an outlaw for the rest of his life.

He thought over the situation for a moment, then said, "I know a way to get the old man. Let's leave this place and then look at the datatext for where he lives."

She started outside with him, waiting while he cautiously checked to make sure they weren't under surveillance. The area around the warehouse was quiet, almost deserted, with litter and dust in the street. The glare of sunlight made him squint, and the heat cooked him as soon as he stepped from the shade.

He gestured for Beaulieu to join him and said, "We don't have to keep our presence a secret now, just our location. As long as we keep moving about the city, it will be hard for them to pinpoint us when I call Sparrow."

"But he'll have snoops on his receiver."

"Perhaps," said 41, breathing the hot air as shallowly as possible to protect his lungs. "But it doesn't matter. He can go through—"

"But he'll be followed. He'll lead them right to us."

41 bared his teeth, feeling better at the prospect of good hunting and certain kills. "Not if we follow the followers."

Beaulieu stared at him and slowly nodded. "I see," she said. "You're very cool when it comes to taking big risks, aren't you?"

"Risk does not mean to me what it means to you."

"You're going to enjoy killing the troopers, aren't you?"

Now she was trying to pry inside his head again. Annoyed, he glared at her. "Don't you want revenge, Doctor?"

"Yes," she said without hesitation. "But it won't bring them back."

Real anger pulsed through him. Why did humans always reach for the easiest misunderstanding? He could have explained to her that revenge cleared the soul of festering, but she would have argued.

"Come," he snapped, and quickened his pace.

The minute hormonal changes of conception brought Melaethia out of vein-burn. Her mind clarified and she found herself locked tightly with the moaning Nefir in the royal bed. How long had she been here, lost in the frenzy?

Red sunlight burned the room through slatted windows, distorting all the colors and shapes in its haze. She blinked, counting the hours, and realized it was late afternoon.

Alarm quickened her. She must go.

Nefir's fangs sank into her shoulder, and the tiny pain of puncture awakened other, older agonies from their numbness. Melaethia shifted against him, shoving his head away.

He growled, gripping her close for the deep pain. She cried out, aware that he was trying to arouse her to new frenzy. But her blood ran cool and silent in her veins. She no longer knew passion, but only exhaustion and the weakness of blood loss and an ever-growing sense of urgency.

She must go.

Again she shoved him. He grunted, panting hard for breath with a raggedness that spoke of his age. He clawed her spine.

The urge to fight him filled her with a last burst of exquisite torment. She could feel it building until the pressure threatened to explode within her. But she fought only herself, not him.

He could sense the responses within her, however, and her control seemed to inflame him. She groped in the tangle of bedclothes for his dagger. No one dared hold a weapon to Nefir, yet she must get away soon before she succumbed again to the mindless frenzy beating inside her.

"*Hegrah!*" shouted Nefir.

She screamed and felt a second conception. Fear coated her like water. Multiple births were a great honor. They could also kill her.

Nefir stroked her face. "Precious one, daughter of Gam, little mother of many. Give me more."

"Great lord, no," she whispered. "Please, I beg for release. Please—"

He lifted his head and laughed in his madness. His eyes were rimmed in red. They held no quarter.

Melaethia's desperate fingers found the blade of his dagger beneath a pillow. She cut herself on it, but its pain shielded her from his.

"Let me go, Great One. Please. Let me rest."

But he wasn't listening. She saw his muscles strain. His claws dug deep into her flesh, holding her in place. Nefir had never sired twin sons before. They would be considered an omen of the gods—a mark of greatness over his reign. And Melaethia saw herself as his consort, honored as no other woman was honored. The whole Empire would lie at her perfumed feet. Her every wish would be gratified. Her sons would be placed first in the line of Nefir's heirs. Her name would be glorified, carved upon the city walls, and proclaimed across the Empire. She would live pampered in her own court. A thousand slaves would attend her every want.

It was beyond a dream, beyond imagining, and yet it was happening. The temptation of such power made her forget her father's views on tyranny, made her forget her own questions and doubts.

She laughed aloud and caressed Nefir's head. "Twins, Great One. Strong sons, blessed by Gam, conceived in the sunlight of Ru. They will make your name shine above all others."

If Nefir had heard her then, if he had faded from the clutches of vein-burn and drawn back, if he had kissed her gently and called for his servants to tend to their injuries, Melaethia would have bound herself to him forever.

But Nefir was lost in his own blood frenzy. Although he had begun to wheeze with exhaustion, he did not release her. And Melaethia suddenly knew bitter disgust. To him she was nothing except a trophy of his own prowess. The current consort would protect her own power base and make sure Melaethia never saw the Pharaon again. If the sons were born and lived, Melaethia could be conveniently killed by the physicians in attendance. Without the Pharaon's protection, she could not survive and he did not even know her name.

She growled in fury and fought him, using claws and teeth, kicking and screaming in an effort to break free. Despite his age, Nefir remained stronger. She whipped the dagger out from beneath the pillow and brandished it in his face.

Nefir's eyes glowed at her, then he struck. The deep pain filled her with such agony she thought she could not live through it. He would never stop. He was mad. He would never stop.

His cry of triumph filled the air.

She plunged the dagger hilt-deep in his vitals. He arched against it, shuddering hard. Then his body sank down upon hers. She heard the choked gurgle in his throat and a long, expelled sigh.

For a moment she lay there pinned beneath him, their blood and passion intermingled. The only heartbeat in the now still chamber was her own.

What had she done?

Killed a god. Killed the Pharaon. Killed him out of lust and panic and stupidity.

At any time the servants and Courtiers of the Bedchamber could enter and find him dead. She whimpered soundlessly and squirmed away from him. The harsh crimson light washed over Nefir's slack face and sightless eyes. It showed the age lines across his cheekbones, the rough skin, the paunch. Just a man now. Just a corpse. He would begin to rot within hours. His amber blood soaked into the embroidered linen.

Sitting up, Melaethia rubbed her nicked arms in numbed panic. She avoided looking at him.

The third conception stirred her.

"No!" she cried out in horror. "No! No!"

But it was done. She pressed her hand to her womb, clawing at her flesh as though to dig out the fertilized cells. Birthing was too difficult; she would surely die if she had to bear three.

Nefir's litter, she thought. Hate washed over her and she rolled off the bed. She knelt naked by the windows and lifted shaking hands to Tees, the goddess of childbirth who was only a myth for children to learn.

What if the Earthers could not cope with multiple birthings? They were ignorant, smelly savages. Their physicians were probably barbarians. Oh, she was a fool, a stupid, conceited fool led by her own pride into disaster.

But she could not stay here, mewling and shivering like a coward forever. It was her own fault this had come to pass. Now it was up to her to get out of the palace before Nefir was discovered. If she was caught for the murder of the Pharaon, not only she but her father, her brother, and all the thousands of their house would be executed. The streets would run with blood.

Don't think about it. Just get out.

Dragging herself upright, she staggered about the opulent chamber and found only remnants of her clothes. Tossing the shredded fabric aside, she dug inside a chest for a plain houserobe of purple cloth. It was embroidered too richly for streetwear, but it was the plainest garment she could find.

She put it on, her slender body lost in its voluminous folds, and found a jeweled belt to gather it at her waist. She pulled the sheets over Nefir, shuddering and averting her eyes as she did so. The eunuchs had orders not to disturb them, but by now it would be all over the Defended City that the Pharaon was locked in vein-burn with a concubine. Heads would have been counted; they would know she was the one. If anyone saw her, she would be detained at once to be hooded and cloistered and examined in case of conception.

Bitterness and fear twisted inside her. She staggered and nearly fell, for she was weak. She needed food and sleep. She did not know how she could possibly escape the Defended City without detection. No guard would order a transport litter for her.

She fought off despair and silently opened the hidden door to the tiny alcove where the Pharaon's women had to wait for his summons. The door leading into the outer corridor had been locked.

Relieved, she wiped her face. An engaged lock meant no guard stood on duty here. Drawing up the hood of the houserobe, she unlocked the door and peered out.

She saw no one in the corridor, but in the distance she could hear voices, running in a low murmur and punctuated by occasional laughter. The courtiers were waiting, gossiping to pass the time. There had been many events scheduled today in the Pharaon's honor, but all must have been canceled when he did not appear.

Carnival was over.

She gasped, clutching herself. Be strong, she told herself.

Starting down the corridor in the opposite direction from the unseen courtiers, she heard the click of a surveillance cam switching on. Drawing the hood down even more, she hurried, twisting down an even smaller service corridor at the first cross passage she came to.

There was no hope of keeping her sense of direction. She changed passageways randomly, always ducking away from any approaching footsteps. Once or twice she collided with servants, who stared at her in surprise, but Melaethia gave them no opportunity to see her face.

To her horror, she found herself walking behind the latticework shading the music pools. Laughter and energetic splashing from the swimmers played counterpoint to the music lessons of the royal children and their mothers.

Melaethia paused to stare through the lattice at them. Vivid colors and bronzed young bodies, smooth and vigorous in the bright wash of sunlight. Slaves in dripping linen plastered to their bodies massaged and oiled the naked limbs of women whose beauty eclipsed Melaethia's. The music paused for corrections from the master, and one child petulantly threw her fluton into the pool with a flashing sizzle of destroyed circuits, bringing laughter from the other pupils and an oath from the master.

Endless luxury . . . chains of silk. With stinging eyes Melaethia drew away and started to hurry on.

A hand grasped her shoulder and spun her around, making her cry out in fright. For a moment she could neither breathe nor see clearly. She had only a confused impression of gold and turquoise trousers ending at the knee, a bare chest supporting a magnificent collar of jewels, and a face, a thin, bronzed face with a merciless slash of a mouth and cold cruel eyes.

Melaethia's mouth opened, but she could not utter a sound.

"What have we here?" he said in his sleek court drawl. "A little *flicket* fluttering toward freedom? No, it is a maiden escaped from her keepers. Do you have a lover, little one? A handsome oparch of the guard who is willing to lose his eyes and tongue for the chance of sampling your favors?"

Melaethia's heart beat so fast her throat felt engorged with blood, choking her so that she could not breathe, could not speak, could not think. Desperately she kept her eyes lowered, holding her head so that the hood left her face shaded.

All hope had left her. The man now grasping her shoulder with fingers like steel was her worst nightmare, the last person she could fool, the one whose name sent shudders through the most secure courtiers. She was lost, truly lost.

He sniffed, and she knew the smell of blood upon her had reached his nostrils. He tipped back her hood with a suddenness that made her flinch. Slowly as though prey to a will stronger than her own, she found herself lifting her gaze to his black one.

"Well, well," said the vaudan. He bared his perfect, pointed teeth. "Have you tired of the Pharaon's bed so quickly, Melaethia? If you are seeking variations, perhaps I can help you."

She spat and twisted in his grasp, but Raumses caught her with his other hand and held her fast despite her struggles.

"No," he said softly. "No escape for you. I know all about your father's plot to undo the Empire and leave Gamael."

She went cold and stopped struggling. Soon he would know something even worse. She no longer saw any need to delay the inevitability of her death.

"Nefir is dead," she said, and had the dubious satisfaction of seeing Raumses' eyes flare wide with shock.

For a moment he stared at her, saying nothing. It was impossible to tell what he was thinking, for no expression at all showed upon his face. She had expected rage, horror. She expected him to strike her, perhaps even slay her on the spot.

Instead Raumses sucked in an audible breath and smiled very, very slightly.

"Excellent!" he said. "Where is he?"

She frowned, not understanding him at all. He was supposed to be Nefir's closest friend, the one man Nefir trusted. Raumses twisted her arm, hurting her.

"Where is he?"

She gasped, for his roughness had reopened a cut on her wrist. "In b-bed. Shut in the chamber."

Raumses narrowed his eyes. "There is time, then. We must keep you out of sight."

"Time for what?"

He hustled her along the corridor, away from the music pools where the children splashed and sang in happy oblivion of their future.

"Have you no grasp of politics? Time, my pretty one, for me to seize the throne first."

Melaethia stumbled and he shoved her on roughly, walking so fast her weak legs could barely keep up. "But there are the heirs—"

Raumses snorted, and then with fresh horror Melaethia understood what he intended. He must have men loyal to him within the military. In minutes he would order assassins to strike the nursery. Cold gorge rose in her throat. She glanced over her shoulder where faint sounds of childish laughter could still be heard.

"Tell me," said Raumses casually. "Will you bear our poor Nefir a child?"

All she could think of was the three within her. Little cells, tiny but soon to grow, fetuses that might kill her if she lived until their birthing. She knew that the blood smeared upon her hid her true scents from Raumses or he would not be asking. By morning her breasts would begin to form; in a few days she would begin to show. She could not hide her condition long.

But she did not have a few days. She had only now, this moment. Raumses would kill her in this very spot if he knew the truth. And she wanted to live.

"I—" Her voice stuck. "I am barren of that honor."

The vaudan laughed, and she realized how stupid the formal words sounded coming from Nefir's murderess.

Oh, *pata*, she thought in despair. I wanted to help you in your cause, not bring down destruction.

They came to a door. Raumses opened it and thrust her inside. She found herself inside a small room.

"What are you going to do with me?" she asked.

He smiled. "You may have many uses. Thank you, pretty one. Perhaps I shall reward you by making you my consort."

He shut the door and engaged the lock. Melaethia pressed her hand against the panel and closed her eyes. He was lying. Sooner or later he would kill her.

The room smelled of water. After a while she wandered about the small space. One end was filled with tall amphoras, all empty. A grate had been set into the center of the floor. She crouched by it, trying to peer down below. She could hear the rush and slap of water, but she could not see it. Melaethia curled her fingers through the grating, wishing she had the strength to lift it and drown herself.

9

Four master architects labored twenty years to build the Defended City. When it was finished and dedicated to the glory of Osan I, he ordered the four men blinded, their tongues cut out, and their hands severed that they should not surpass its design.

—History of the First Dynasty

Waterlogged: first you shriveled a little; then you shriveled a lot; then your skin turned white providing it wasn't dyed blue, in which case it turned a queer shade of sick lavender; then you wrinkled all over; then your skin began to smell; then you felt like you were rotting away.

Caesar didn't feel quite that bad, but it was close. When he woke up maybe three hours ago, he'd found himself with a pounding headache, a feeling of having had his guts wrung inside out, and dire thirst exacerbated by the fact that he was wedged chest-deep in a drainage tunnel with a grate letting in sunshine overhead. The light was welcome despite the fact that it reflected off the water in jittery little flecks that kept him half blinded.

He had tried to pull himself free without success. As far as he could tell it was his tanks that were caught, but his left arm was twisted and doubled back behind him and his right couldn't reach the release catch despite all the twisting and tugging, straining and grunting, he'd gone through trying to squirm loose. He couldn't reach the wristband on his left arm either. He figured by now Kelly and the squad had finished up, written him off, and gone home.

Caesar glowered, letting his chin sink closer to the water. He hoped Phila would turn up, but there'd been no sign of her—alive or dead.

He'd already gone through the panicked stage, the cursing stage, the awed stage that he was still alive, the morose stage, and the self-pity stage. Now all he felt was mad.

He figured he had a few options left; two were that he could stay here until his skin rotted off his bones or until he starved to death. He wasn't going to drink this gunk he was immersed in, no sir, not even if his tongue dried to a little sliver of fuzz and stuck to the roof of his mouth. And he sure as hell wasn't going to die in the sewers of the wig-heads, dyed blue and alone.

He'd lost his face mask and his gear bag. But he still had one soft explosive gel pack stashed inside his wet suit where he could reach it. All he had to do was dig it out, toss it through that grating, and shake himself loose.

The trouble was, he was liable to shake loose the whole roof of the tunnel and bury himself in here.

Caesar sighed and wiped the sweat off his face. Maybe he wasn't going to shrivel up completely; maybe his skin would melt with the wet suit and form a new synthetic. He would own the processing rights and become a rich man.

"I'm going nuts," he said aloud. "Great, now I'm talking to myself. Next I'll be screaming for help. And all that'll get me is a wig-head and fourteen centimeters of blaster run down my windpipe."

A noise, caught and amplified by the water, silenced him. Caesar shrank closer to the wall, grimacing as a fresh cramp caught him. He listened hard. It was something overhead, moving around the grating. A voice, indistinct but Salukan. Then silence.

Caesar was starting to breathe again when a shadow fell across him. He glanced up and saw a woman silhouetted in the sunlight. She crouched upon the grating and curled her fingers through it.

For a moment Caesar thought she'd seen him. Then, when

she did nothing at all, he told himself to stop being a numb-nut. Kelly should be long gone by now, so who cared if the wig-heads found out a few Earthers had strolled through their capital city? Execution had to be better than rotting down here.

If they executed him. *If* they didn't put him through the mind sieve first. Caesar figured he could cause enough trouble to get some dumb trooper excited enough to shoot him.

"Hey!" he said in Saluk before he could talk himself out of it. "Hey, you up there!"

The woman jerked back and vanished. Exasperated, Caesar waited a moment.

"Come on," he said, sounding more pathetic than he meant to. "I'm stuck down here. Give me a hand."

She peered down through the grate, but obviously didn't see him. "Who is there?"

"Me," said Caesar. "I've been here for hours and I'd like to dry out. Can you lift that grate?"

She mumbled something he didn't catch, but she did manage to shift the heavy grate to one side.

"Terrific," said Caesar with fresh enthusiasm. "Now, reach down so I can grab your hand."

She paused, peering down again. This time she saw him. He got a better look at her as well from this angle. Caesar swallowed hard, and felt his customary charm with the ladies drying up. She was shaved bald as an onion and had a shiner on one eye that was a dandy.

Still, she didn't look like she was armed. And she hadn't raised an alarm yet.

She frowned. "You're Yllrian. What are you doing down there?"

Caesar could have kissed her, bald head and all. Maybe his disguise was better than he thought. He grinned. "It's a long story . Give me a hand. Please?"

"You lack respect." But she lowered her hand to him just the same.

Caesar grabbed her wrist. Her fingers were strong. She pulled, but nothing happened.

"Damn!" Caesar strained with all his might. The pain in

his left shoulder made sweat pop out all over him. "Keep pulling!"

It wasn't going to happen. He was stuck here forever.

And then, without warning, he came free with a harsh scrape of his tanks upon the stone and a burst of agony from his arm. He dropped his grasp on her wrist and sank under the water. But he fought his way up again, dragging in a ragged breath, and flailed one-handedly until he caught her wrist again.

She pulled and he climbed, and for a while he teetered half in and half out of the hole. The edge of the grate poked him savagely in the armpit. He swore and finally managed to flounder belly-flat onto the floor beside her.

"Yusus," he groaned, groping until he found the release catch. The tanks finally fell off, and he rolled over in relief.

"Who are you?" demanded the Salukan girl.

He waited until he got his breath back and the wrenching agony in his left arm quieted a bit. He felt gingerly between his elbow and wrist and found nothing but bruises. The break was above the elbow, and when he touched it Kloper charges seemed to go off behind his eyes.

When the world stopped being a sick shade of yellow and became normal again, he found the girl kneeling beside him.

"You're hurt," she said.

He nodded, feeling too woozy to talk. She gestured at the small room, bare except for a stack of dusty old metal jars in one corner.

"There is nothing to give you. I am locked in here. I am Melaethia."

"Caesar," he said, forgetting what his cover name was supposed to be. Some damned snarl in the throat with a couple of consonant twists. It didn't matter now anyway.

She frowned, mouthing his name to herself.

"Locked in?" he said, beginning to think again. "Why?"

She drew back. An expression of pride and fear crossed her face. "I have killed the Pharaon. Soon I shall die."

Caesar grinned, deciding that with some hair on her head she wouldn't look half bad. "Why, honey, a little-bitty thing like you? Congratulations. I'll bet this place is swarming like an ant den.''

She blinked, looking bewildered. *''Den?''* she repeated, giving it the wrong inflection.

''Never mind.'' He managed to climb to his feet with her help. ''Thanks. Stand back now. See if you can get behind some of those jars.''

''The amphoras? Why?''

He pulled out his gel packet and hefted it in his hand. ''Because I'm going to unlock the door.''

Melaethia stared at him. ''Are you an assassin? Yllrians are not permitted inside the Defended City. Did you swim beneath the—''

''Yeah,'' said Caesar impatiently. ''Go on. Take cover. This is a lot of punch for one small door.''

She shoved a couple of amphoras into place and crouched behind them. Caesar eyed the structure fittings of the door and the size of the room. The door would blow out fine; he just hoped the ceiling wouldn't come down with it.

Squeezing the packet for ten seconds to activate the internal detonator, Caesar tossed it at the door and threw himself flat.

The concussion picked him up and slammed him down at the same time as a tremendous roar rocked his eardrums. He felt the belch of heat, then dust and debris choked the air.

Caesar cautiously lifted his head. His ears were ringing and he felt numb all over, but it had been a nice, neat little blast, just the way he liked it. The door and the wall that had held it were both gone.

Caesar walked over to it and peered out through the haze. In the distance he heard the shrill whoop of an alarm and some shouting. He smiled and glanced over his shoulder at Melaethia, who was peeking over the top of an amphora with enormous eyes.

''You coming?'' he asked.

Without hesitation she got to her feet and joined him.

He took her hand and she winced as though it hurt. He looked her over more closely. Whoever had given her the black eye had done a thorough job. Caesar bristled. He didn't believe in beating up women. If you had to shoot one who was shooting at you, that was different. But all a bashing did was spoil their looks, and this one needed all the good looks she could get.

"I guess the guards roughed you up when they caught you," he said by way of offering sympathy.

She frowned at him. "No."

It was his turn to be puzzled. "How'd you get the bruises?"

She touched her cheek and suddenly smiled in comprehension. "I see. This is nothing. The Pharaon—"

She didn't finish her sentence.

Caesar nodded. "Yeah. No wonder you snuffed him."

"Snuffed?"

"Killed him. You said you did."

Her face drew taut and ugly with emotion. She averted her gaze. "Yes. I—I had to."

"Hey," he said gently, putting his hand on her shoulder. "It's rough, the first time you have to kill someone."

"You do not understand," she said unsteadily. "All my life he has been a symbol of supreme power. I had never even seen him face-to-face until yesterday."

"Honey," said Caesar, cautiously easing up to a cross passageway and peering along it. "Emperors, presidents, and pharaons all put their pants on one leg at a time—providing they wear pants and they got legs. Life is sacred, sure, but your Pharaon wasn't. From what I hear, he was a two-faced, lying, egotistical squat."

That made her look at him. Awe spread across her face. "You *are* an assassin. You speak of him so insultingly, yet casually. He meant nothing to you."

"Nope," said Caesar cheerfully.

"Are you going to kill me?"

Caesar's rapid stride faltered. "Why the hell should I?"

"Because I have kept you from your job. Now you will not be paid for—"

"Look, Melly. Get this straight. I'm not here to do in the Pharaon. I took a wrong turn and got sucked down the drain. That's all. Now I want to get out of here just as fast as I can before we connect with whoever's coming to check on my little blast back there. Whoops. Strike a trot."

He whipped back from a corner where he saw troopers approaching double-time and shooed Melaethia back the way they'd come. This was stupid. He couldn't run around like a rat in a maze, hoping luck would eventually lead him outside.

Darting down a cross passageway, he said, "You could give me a few hints on the best way out of here. You know the gambit: I do you a favor and you do me a favor."

"I'm lost," said Melaethia.

Caesar's blood pressure shot up several notches. He hated adrenaline rushes on empty stomachs. Swearing, he jerked Melaethia around a corner, but a distant shout told him it was too late.

"They've spotted us. Now we're in for it."

He ran, wincing as every step jolted his injured arm. Melaethia kept beside him, panting for breath. Neither of them was in any shape to outrun troopers. Caesar quickened his pace, resisting the urge to glance back. The troopers shouted again. They sounded closer. In a few seconds it would be shooting time, and he wasn't armed.

Caesar frowned, trying to think of some options.

Melaethia suddenly darted away from him. "This way!"

A blaster on long-range scored the wall between them. Caesar fought the instinctive reflex to dodge back and forced himself to follow Melaethia in her flowing purple robe.

"Here!" she said. "I recognize this area. Through here. Quickly."

Another shot scorched the air just above Caesar's right shoulder. He didn't look to see where she was pointing, and he didn't waste time. He dove through the door she had pulled open and found himself in pitch-darkness. His knee hit something sharp and solid. Yelping, he staggered to one side and sank down, biting the soft inside of his lip to keep himself from swearing long and hard.

She rustled past, tapping his shoulder as she went. "Quickly," she whispered. "Make no sound. Come."

He rose and groped until he managed to catch the back of her robe. He hung on to it, stumbling after her in total blindness.

"Where are we?"

"Ssh."

"But where *are* we?"

She stopped so that he bumped into her. Her hand gripped his throat, startling him into silence.

"We are in the storage rooms of the seraglio."

"The *what*—"

She gave him a warning shake, but he'd already heard a sound ahead of them and shut up. Someone was coming this way, and at any time the troopers following them would burst in. They were trapped.

She pulled him to one side, and this time he went with her willingly, trusting her superior nocturnal vision. He found himself stuffed among racks of clothes smelling of perfume and dusty fibers. It was all he could do not to sneeze. But he rustled deeper into the clothes, and held his breath as a light stabbed on, illuminating the storeroom. He could see nothing but the robes hanging around him in a staggering array of colors.

Troopers tramped through perfunctorily, halting in the storeroom. Caesar held his breath, willing himself to make no sound. This was no good, he knew. As soon as the wigheads searched, this hiding place would fold. His fingers tightened into a fist.

He heard the clash of salutes upon armored chests.

"Get out," snapped a thin, ill-tempered voice. "Troopers are not permitted in this area."

"We must," protested another. "We are following two—"

"No searching! This area is barred."

To Caesar's disbelief, the troopers filed out. Caesar emerged warily in case one or two had dropped behind, but they were gone. He shook his head in scorn. Backing out of a harem just because it wasn't considered nice to go in was a pretty lax way of securing prisoners. But he wasn't going to complain.

Melaethia appeared from her hiding place behind a tall chest. She carried an orange robe over her arm and thrust it at Caesar.

"It's hooded. Put it on. They won't dare search deeper into

the women's courts until later, perhaps not at all unless the vaudan has the eunuchs put to death."

"Why?" asked Caesar, struggling out of his wet suit and into the robe. It was certainly cooler. "What's going on? A palace coup?"

Melaethia stared at him. "Don't you know? Aren't you part of it?"

His head popped out and he shook the robe down around him. "Do I look like I know what's going on?"

"You are very strange for an Yllrian," she said. "I do not think you are . . ."

Her voice trailed off and a frightened look crossed her face.

There was no point in denying what she'd finally guessed. Caesar said, "That's right. I'm really a human."

He tensed, ready for her to turn on him and sound the alarm, but instead she gripped his arm excitedly.

"You are with the Earthers who have come to help my father escape Gamael. How—"

Caesar frowned. "Arnaht?"

"Yes, yes! I am Melaethia, his daughter. I want to leave with my father." She paused and a look of defiant pride crossed her narrow face. "I carry the Pharaon's child. I wanted to bear it among you Earthers, to shame him. But now he is dead, and I do not see how we can escape the Defended City in time."

Caesar had no interest in politics, but he understood immediately what she had done and what it could mean. He had to get her out, all right. The only problem was, how?

In the distance the sound of gunfire and screaming sent Caesar whirling.

Melaethia shook her hands in agitation. "Assassins in the nursery. Raumses is a—"

"Never mind." Caesar grabbed her arm and pulled her back the way they'd come. "We can't go to ground here. And hiding's no good anyway. We've got to get out or we'll be left behind."

"How did you get into the Defended City? Can we not retrace that route?"

He wished with all his heart they could. ''Not unless you can breathe water.''

At the door, he checked for all-clear, but another squad of troopers ran by, sending Caesar and Melaethia back inside the storeroom. They weren't seen, and Caesar eased out his breath. This was no good. The whole place was too hot, and their odds were looking worse all the time. He needed a weapon, dammit.

''Now!'' he said, and darted into the corridor. ''We've got to get outside. Start giving directions.''

Ahead, a strong rattle of gunfire punctuated by the occasional whine of plasma made him pull up. The army, obviously, was fighting itself. Probably it had split, with one faction supporting the vaudan's takeover and the rest resisting the whole idea. Good. The more confused things got, the better chance he and Melaethia had of slipping through a crack somewhere.

Caesar listened until he was sure the battle sounds were fading. The survivors went in the opposite direction, and Caesar hurried forward. Easing around a bend in the corridor, he stepped over a handful of sprawled courtiers and as many guards. Snatching up a dagger and a couple of blasters, he nodded at Melaethia, who was doing the same.

She gestured. ''If we take the left turning, it leads straight to the audience chamber. Beyond that is an exit to the parade ground.''

''Perfect.'' Caesar checked the charge on his weapons. High, practically unused. His spirits rose. ''Ready?''

She smiled.

Caesar tucked his left hand through his belt to help support his arm and winced. It was beginning to really hurt from all this running around. He started forward. ''Keep close and pray for luck. We're going to need all we can get.''

Across Byiul, Kelly felt his knees jellifying on him again. He pushed himself out of the stream of pedestrians and paused to rest in the doorway of a closed shop. Most people kept out of his way, giving respect to his yellow *sulla*, but the heat and loss of blood were getting to him. The cloth had a peculiar weave to it that allowed him to see out, but no one to see in. He worried about bloodstains soaking through, but a lightweight framework resting on his shoulders kept the garment standing away from him. The hem dragged the ground, but he couldn't help that.

He'd managed to leave the temple compound unchallenged. The surveillance monitor had left, much to his relief, and nothing appeared to be on his tail now.

He closed his eyes a moment, waiting for the shaky chills to go away. All he needed was the wound bandaged and one of Beaulieu's wonder drugs and he'd be fine. In the meantime, Beaulieu was a long ways off and time was running out. He checked his chron.

He'd run out of options. He had to break silence and call for help. The risk had become necessary.

Using the pulse code wouldn't work, since they'd set all their wristbands to allow only Caesar's frequency to come through. Kelly's message had to be verbal, and it had to be short so a surveillance net wouldn't trace it back to this spot.

That was all right. He didn't have the breath for long speeches.

He rested a moment longer, aware that as soon as he made the call he'd have to change locations. It was easier to leave his eyes closed, but as soon as he sensed that reality was fading out he forced himself erect and pressed the send switch.

"Kelly to 41. Come in, 41. I need help. Do you copy?"

No answer. Kelly waited, unwilling to accept silence.

"Kelly to 41. Come in."

Nothing.

Maybe 41 was too cautious to break transmission silence. Maybe 41 couldn't answer because he'd been caught in a trap similar to the one that nearly got Kelly on the quay. Maybe he was already outside the city perimeter, and it was too far to come back in.

Kelly stared at his wristband, fighting off another chill and trying not to let despair engulf him. Suicide mission, he thought bleakly. You knew that when you volunteered. Why do you always think you can beat the odds?

He had to start moving. With a groan Kelly pushed himself away from the doorway. He turned down a different street, still heading generally in the same direction. He was strictly on his own now; he'd better keep sharp.

Over in northeast Byiul, in the industrial section where the grinding roar of freight transports rumbled along an overhead street, 41's wristband nudged him with a single electronic pulse. At once he whipped off the walkway into a narrow alley.

Beaulieu was walking maybe ten meters behind him in the crowd. 41 glanced back and gestured. She nodded and ambled on ahead of him, then paused as though watching a massive cargo shuttle set itself on hover with its jets whipping the air while it dumped its contents into a storage tank with a deafening clang of hard liquid.

41 cupped his wristband with his hand and listened carefully to Kelly's voice calling for help. Inside, 41 felt as though a constricting band had been cut away. He grinned to himself, making sure his wristband's tracer was homing on Kelly's signal.

Just like any surveillance net in the city, he thought, and stopped grinning. Kelly must really need him to take a risk like this.

41 started to answer, then stopped himself. A one-way communication might slip through the nets. A two-way would definitely be picked up. In his service as a mercenary, he'd seen green recruits make that mistake. They never lived to learn from it.

Kelly called again, sounding desperate or hurt. 41 frowned at the urgency in Kelly's voice. Time was running out, and he had not yet been able to set his own trap for Sparrow. But that no longer mattered. He had to reach Kelly quickly.

It was all he could do not to answer back. 41 kept his wristband tracer activated. It would help him pinpoint Kelly's location, even if Kelly moved.

Beaulieu was pretending to mend her duffle strap when 41 joined her. He kept his eyes moving constantly, watching for informers who earned pocket money by reporting anyone suspicious on the streets, watching for surveillance monitors, watching for troopers.

''What is it?'' Beaulieu asked. ''Change of plan?''

''Kelly is alive.''

Her face lit up and she surged to her feet. ''He is? How do you—''

41 gripped her arm to calm her down. ''He just called for help. I'll handle it. You meet Sparrow.''

She opened her mouth, but he gave her no chance to speak. ''Go in carefully. Remember that he probably has betrayed us and don't fall into his trap. Watch your back. And get there early so that you can hide and watch who comes.''

Beaulieu nodded impatiently. ''I know how to do all that. What about—''

''We can't both go,'' said 41. He already knew how he could get to Kelly fast, but it was risky, too risky for both of them to try.

''He must be injured to break transmission silence.'' Beaulieu pulled out her medikit and handed it to him. ''You'll need this. Don't use anything marked with a yellow tab.''

41 took the medikit in surprise. He had expected her to argue, to insist on coming along, to be a fool.

''Go on,'' she said impatiently. ''I'll deal with Sparrow.''

It seemed backward suddenly, him going off with the medikit and she making the rendezvous. He hesitated, aware to his own consternation that he was worried about separating from her.

There was no choice. She had to work, not be protected. He stowed the medikit inside his *chunta* and nodded to her in respect.

''Watch yourself,'' he said again.

She smiled, her dark eyes capable and unafraid. ''Just bring Kelly home.''

10

Friendship is useful and rare. Guard it above rubies.
—Saluk proverb

41 hit a ground-eating stride that carried him swiftly through the slower-moving crowd until he was well out of sight of Beaulieu. Checking for any monitors, he ducked into a service alley choked with loaders and crates. It was momentarily cleared of any Salukan workers other than an ambulatory drone switched off to conserve power and propped in the seat of a loader. 41 shrugged off the duffles of gear he carried. Swiftly he pulled out an expensive pair of linen trousers and a severely cut tunic with the symbol of Juvanne House embroidered in silver thread.

He changed clothes behind a stack of crates, discarding his *chunta* and dirty headdress. Combing through his blond hair with his fingers, he let it hang free and undisguised. In fine clothes and wearing the symbol of the Pharaon's own house, his mixed breeding became less objectionable. He did not paint his face as a sign of even greater importance.

One quick twist of his dagger, and the crate lock shorted out. 41 opened it and tossed in the duffles and the jammer. He saved only the datatext and Beaulieu's medikit. Tucking these under his arm, he fitted his Brud into his pocket and left the alley from the opposite end just as delivery workers emerged from a building.

They stared at him in plain curiosity, but 41 ignored them. One of them inclined in respect as he passed.

41 flicked him a gesture. "Leave your names with our Treasury," he said in high Saluk, drawling out the tops of his vowels as only the upper classes could. "We intend to buy your delivery company. You will be hired with better contracts."

They inclined again, blank-faced with astonishment, and 41 strode on briskly.

As soon as he reached a canal, he stopped at a quay and flung up his hand in summons. Two launches jostled to reach him first, but 41 ignored them. He wanted an aircab. Expensive, exclusively for the hire of the best classes, and the fastest transportation in Byiul, aircabs were uncommon. The quay porter—looking anxious to please—called one and it arrived a couple of minutes later.

41 knew the custom was usually to sneer at the aircab's appearance and demand another. No member of a major house ever accepted the first thing offered. But he couldn't afford to carry the act to its fullest; he didn't have time.

He gestured satisfaction, and the porter's expression fell in disappointment. No doubt he had a kickback arrangement with the second aircab he would have summoned. 41 did not tip him either.

Climbing inside, 41 wrinkled his nose at the cab's musty smell. It hovered a moment above the ground.

"Destination, domei?"

41's wristband was still tracing Kelly's location. "Southwest across the city. Extra tip if you get there fast."

"As the domei wishes."

The aircab lifted straight up and swept over the rooftops in a tight spiral that curled through 41's stomach.

41 looked out, watching Byiul flash beneath him. Aircabs apparently had tightly restricted airspace. They skimmed the rooftops and tilted between tall buildings rather than going above them. A shuttle roared by overhead, dwarfing them with its size, and tossed them in its airstream. Monitors

floated outside an occasional window or hovered over pedestrians.

They left the industrial quarter and passed over a squalid residential area. In minutes, however, the streets began to look more affluent. They skimmed a wide berth around the Defended City. 41 noticed larger air traffic doing the same. It must be illegal to fly over. From this angle he spotted artillery muzzles from the towers rising above the Defended City, ready to enforce that law if necessary.

"Which quarter, domei?" asked the driver.

41 checked his locator. "Maintain your direction."

"No games, domei," said the driver in sudden suspicion. "It's my license if we do anything illegal—"

41 placed the wide-bore muzzle of his Brud against the driver's neck. "Land in Tupsetshe Park."

The driver stiffened, and the aircab did an involuntary bobble. "That's not allowed. Stolat Quay—"

"Not the quay," said 41 firmly. "Land in the park."

"Domei, please—"

41 jabbed the gun harder against the driver's neck, thumping against its protective cartilage. "One shot is enough to sever your head from your body," he said. "Follow orders."

The driver swooped over the park and dropped swiftly to a low hover. "I'll lose my license for this," he said angrily. "A monitor will copy my number and—"

41 hit him at the base of his neck, and the driver slumped over. Lunging over the seat, 41 hit the hatch toggle and tumbled the man out. He flopped upon the ground in an unconscious sprawl. 41 climbed into the cockpit and put his hands on the controls just as a monitor bobbed into place before the aircab.

"You are in violation of city ordinance 111-R-50," it said over the aircab's communication system. "You will—"

41 pulled the aircab off hover and opened the throttle. He clipped the monitor and had the satisfaction of seeing it spin out of control. It fell into the canal with a small, muffled explosion that sent up a spume of water and caused a launch to veer into the path of another.

Baring his teeth in satisfaction, 41 sent the aircab soaring.

* * *

In Nostru Quarter a contingent of troopers blocked the street ahead. Pedestrians were ordered to form lines. Kelly staggered to a halt. So his transmission hadn't slipped through the net. He looked around, grimacing against another chill. Maybe he could head east and avoid the blockade, but that would put him in the wrong direction.

His chron, however, told him that he could go in any direction he pleased. He would never be able to cross the city in time to rejoin the others now.

"Pardon, dama," said a gruff voice respectfully, startling Kelly. "Step aside and join the line."

Kelly complied, but his heart began to beat too fast. He drew his Brud and held it inside the concealment of the *sulla*. He would take out as many troopers as he could and save one last slug for himself. They weren't going to peel his mind apart ever again in interrogation.

An aircab flew overhead, whipping dust into the air and causing the oparch in charge of the search to wave it off angrily.

A richly dressed couple in front of Kelly protested loudly against being detained. Kelly glared at them, for the oparch came over to them in person. Kelly tried to edge back, but a trooper stopped him.

"No moving please, dama. The heat is strong, but we will not keep you long."

Kelly's mouth was dry. He made a vague gesture and remained silent. There was no way he could achieve a falsetto that would fool anyone. Meanwhile, the oparch had finished with the wealthy couple and released them.

He came to Kelly and inclined. "Your identity card, please."

Kelly did nothing. He had not thought to steal Daria's card, and his own would not help him while he was in this disguise. Men did not wear *sullas*.

"Dama?" said the oparch impatiently. "I regret the necessity for this inconvenience, but if you will not produce your identity card we must search you."

Sweat poured off Kelly. Still, he said nothing.

The oparch backed up a step and drew his blaster. "Step aside."

Two other troopers came hurrying to flank Kelly. He moved out of line while the crowd shrank away.

"Remove the *sulla*," said the oparch.

Someone gasped. It was like demanding a woman remove her clothes in public. Kelly tightened his grip on his weapon, getting the placement of the troopers in his mind. With one hand he pulled the cord near his cheek. The top folds of the *sulla* opened and fell about his shoulders, revealing his short black hair spiked with sweat and his painted but definitely non-Salukan face.

Sounds of angry consternation broke out amidst the crowd. The troopers drew their blasters, and the oparch fairly glowed with excitement.

"An Earther!" He gestured at a youthful aide still in a hairlock. "Contact the regiment Mailord immediately—"

Kelly shot him through the chest, sending him staggering back into the aide, who caught him reflexively. One trooper on Kelly's left seized his arm, but Kelly was too quick for them. He squeezed off two shots, right and left at point-blank range, and ran as they crumpled to the ground.

Shouts rang out, and Kelly heard the flat whine of blaster fire. He ran into the thick of the crowd, which screamed and scattered in confusion. A hillman pulled a dagger on him, and Kelly shot him, elbowing his way past two other civilians who tried to block his path.

But there was nowhere to run to, and his legs were leaden and clumsy. Even the current rush of adrenaline couldn't keep him going far. Blaster fire raked down a youth near Kelly, and with fresh screams the crowd threw themselves flat upon the ground. Kelly's ruse was over.

He whirled, skidding around on one knee, and the Brud bucked hot and lethal in his hand, sending troopers toppling. But he was in the open now with the nearest alley too many steps away; he had seconds, perhaps not even that long, until they mowed him down.

The rough bark of another, unsilenced Brud firing from somewhere to his left sent Kelly's heart leaping with fresh hope. His message had gotten through to 41 after all, and 41 had risked his neck to come back for him. Kelly grinned to himself, feeling fresh strength.

He finished his clip and threw himself flat beside a dead civilian while he thumbed the button to eject the spent clip. Cramming a fresh load in the Brud, he looked around desperately for 41 and spotted him firing from the cover of the alley.

"Kelly!" yelled 41, and waved. Blaster cross fire hit the corner of the building, sending 41 staggering back, but in a moment he was shooting again.

The last trooper went down.

Kelly picked himself up, feeling a rush of light-headedness, and ran toward 41 on legs that felt like knotted rags. Just short of the alley, Kelly staggered and would have fallen had 41 not grabbed him.

41 dragged him up and slammed him against the wall, propping him there with his elbow while he scanned the street. "More troopers coming," he said without greeting. "Don't faint. I can't shoot and carry you."

Kelly nodded, sucking in a deep breath and fighting off the black ravelings at the edges of his vision while 41 fired off another round. 41 ejected his spent clip and reloaded with crisp efficiency.

"Come," he said, gripping Kelly's arm. "Down this way."

Kelly suppressed a groan and did his best to push himself along, but his progress was erratic and slow. He couldn't see well because the alley was spinning around him, and his feet seemed to be a kilometer away. 41 kept shoving him along, glancing back frequently.

"I hope," said Kelly, panting, "that you've got a good hiding place close by. I'm in no shape for a footrace."

41 grunted. His tawny eyes kept moving. He spotted a monitor swooping down upon them from overhead. 41 shot it, sending it exploding into a thousand shattered bits.

Without warning he shoved Kelly against the wall and snaked past him to the corner, pressing himself flat and peering around as though he expected to get his blond head shot off.

"No sight-seeing," he said. "No personal contacts. Those were our orders. You screwed up, Kelly. How bad are you hurt?"

Kelly closed his eyes, savoring the brief moment of rest. "Knife cut. I seem to keep leaking . . ."

41 roused him by pulling him away from the wall. "Quick," he said. "Kelly!"

The black ravelings were beginning to weave together across Kelly's vision. A heavy, sucking weariness pulled at his legs. With a supreme effort he shook off the temptation to succumb.

"I'm wide," he said, blinking fiercely.

41 gripped Kelly by the cheekbones and glared into his eyes. It was a hold similar to the one Daria had used on him, but this time he felt his mind clear. Amazed, he stared at 41, but before he could speak, a blaster scorched him.

Kelly and 41 scrambled around the corner out of the alley.

"Too close," breathed Kelly.

Then he saw the aircab sitting in the street with a cluster of curious civilians around it. 41 dropped his arm and ran forward, brandishing his weapon. The civilians scattered, shouting for troopers. 41 hit the hatch and climbed in, leaving Kelly to struggle after him.

Six meters to the aircab.

Heat was enveloping Kelly, burning over the pain that throbbed through his gut.

Four meters.

He wasn't tracking in a straight line. Keep going. Just keep going. The open hatch yawned like a haven. He could see 41 fitting himself in the cockpit, reaching for the controls.

Three meters.

He had nothing left. His pulse thumped inside his skull; his breath sawed in and out. He could feel his last reserves draining. No more kick. Nothing left to call on.

Keep going, dammit.

One meter.

Shouts from behind him. The whine of blasters overlaid by the Brud's crashing recoil. Kelly frowned, his mind streaking off on a tangent. Why wasn't 41 using his silencer?

It doesn't matter. Keep going.

Kelly hit something solid and belatedly realized it was the side of the aircab. He heard 41 shout, saw 41 slump on the other side of the aircab.

Anger cleared Kelly's swimming head. He swung around with his gun in his hand and sprayed the approaching squad with bullets, longing for a big diehard plasma rifle instead. But the Brud did its work, although more were coming from the other side.

Kelly climbed inside the aircab. The opposite hatch hung half open, with 41's head and shoulders slumped inside.

"41!" shouted Kelly. "Don't you dare be dead!"

41's blond head moved slightly, and relief burst through Kelly. He grabbed 41's shoulders and heaved. 41's dead weight didn't budge. Kelly sank back, gasping for breath. For a moment his mind burned with panic. He couldn't get 41 inside.

"41!" he shouted. "Wake up. You have to wake up. Come on!"

41 didn't stir. His tunic smoked slightly from the blaster burn he'd taken. Kelly could smell the mingled stench of cooked flesh and cloth.

And more troopers were coming, from both sides now. In moments they'd surround the aircab. Kelly had to get the aircab off the ground now, or there was no chance left.

"41!" he said, gripping the operative once again.

He heaved with all his might, straining past his limits until 41's body cleared the hatchway. As 41's legs dropped with a thud upon the carpeted floor, a great gout of blood came out of Kelly. He slumped in the seat, chills running under the fire, and pressed his hands to his abdomen. His head felt light as though it floated somewhere on the ceiling, but the rest of him felt increasingly cold as though his body were congealing in ice.

Stay calm, he told himself. He shuddered, fighting his own failing body, and managed to hit the hatch controls. The hatches closed, and a low whine from the engine told him it had already been started up. The aircab had a simple operating system. Kelly groped his way to the throttle and steering, leaving blood smeared everywhere. He touched LIFT, and the aircab shot into the air, rocketing up too fast and too straight, but leaving the troopers behind. Blaster fire bounced harmlessly off the hull for a couple of minutes, then they soared beyond range.

Kelly's hands slipped off the steering. His eyes closed. He was so tired, so cold.

"Kelly."

Somehow he dragged his eyes open, not certain if he had heard his name or dreamed it.

"Kelly."

41's voice, hoarse and nearly unrecognizable, grated over his name. Kelly did not move, could not move. He stared through the windshield at cobalt sky.

Finally he spoke. "Can you fly this, 41?"

He heard no reply, but he couldn't be sure because his hearing kept fading in and out. His eyes closed again, and this time he didn't fight so hard to keep them open. He was tired.

41 lifted himself in the passenger end of the aircab with a groan. He clutched Kelly's arm, rousing him. Kelly heard him panting with pain. Sympathy rolled through Kelly beneath the fog. Blaster burns meant growing a lot of new skin.

"Hurt?" he whispered.

41's hand dropped off his arm. "Hell, yes, it hurts," he growled. "Open the medikit."

Kelly lapsed again, no longer much interested in anything. The aircab bobbled roughly. Kelly opened his eyes in time to see a vast wing sweep by over them with perhaps a couple of meters clearance. They flopped again in the jet wake, and angry static crackled over the comm.

Kelly frowned. Reckless piloting. Someone should have the controls. "I wanna sleep," he said.

41 punched his arm, jolting him. "Wake up! Open the kit. We need the—"

His voice twisted off in pain.

Kelly struggled against his cold lethargy. Are you going to die because you didn't try hard enough? he asked himself. Another part of him, the heavy, slowing part, no longer cared. But Kelly reached out, groping across the seat beside him. His hand bumped into hard plastic . . . the datatext folded into its case. Half beneath it was Beaulieu's slim kit. Kelly's hand curved around it in wonder. Inside were good things, things that would take the pain away, take the cold away, take the fog away. He smiled, pleased that he had found it.

But he made no move to open it until he heard 41's choked, bitten-off moan. Kelly frowned. Blaster burns hurt, he remembered. Hurt a lot. Hurt as much as being slagged. He should do something for 41.

Gritting his teeth, Kelly managed to pick up the kit and pull it into his bloody lap. He opened it, blinking against the blurriness of his vision, and concentrated long enough to open a pressure bandage. Shaky application to his flesh brought small but instant relief as the surface anesthetic spread into his skin, and the edges of the slash pulled together. He fumbled through the row of neat tabs, and the cloudiness in his mind focused on green.

A long-ago drill echoed in his head: GREEN FOR PRIMARY FIRST AID.

Start with green. When your mind was clear, you could make the proper decision about the rest of the drugs available.

He swallowed the tablet and slumped back in his seat, ignoring the warning beep on the control board. After a few seconds, although he had only the vaguest grasp of elapsed time, the fog began to thin and his woolly thoughts did not drift quite so much. He felt the effects running through his body, spreading through his limbs in queer, cold darts of chemical reaction, driving away the weakness.

The control board continued to beep, with a louder, more insistent noise. Kelly wiped the film of perspiration from his face and finally paid attention to it. He saw a tall building looming directly ahead, and panic slammed through him. Gripping the steering, he sent the aircab veering sharply, rolling it so that her belly skimmed the windows of the building. He glimpsed a startled face at one of the windows, then the aircab soared in an uncontrolled arc over a broad canal and Kelly found himself looking down at the elaborate spires and towers of the Defended City.

The comm squawled. "WARNING! YOU HAVE VIOLATED IMPERIAL AIRSPACE. LAND OR BE DISINTEGRATED. WARNING!"

The aircab bucked and bobbled in Kelly's hands. He realized they'd hit some kind of signal net that was fouling the aircab's electronic circuits. The master computer web governing controls and engine could short out at any moment, crashing them.

Kelly swore aloud. Of all the stupid, brainless things he could have done, flying into the Defended City had to be the worst.

Artillery cannons on a nearby tower swiveled, and Kelly's skin crawled. He knew a disintegrator cannon when he saw one. He didn't want to end his days as a few bits of scattered neutrinos.

"What is it?" asked 41, his voice hoarse with pain. "What's wrong?"

Kelly handed him a green tablet. "Swallow this, then reload your Brud. We're about to land."

11

A woman has more strength in her heart than a man in his sword arm.

—from the Scroll of Tees

The throne room was paneled with sheets of solid gold that reflected light from a multitude of skylights over head. High noon must be blinding, Caesar thought as he hurried across the spacious expanse of polished stone floors veined with green and scarlet. The throne itself glowed with emeralds and rubies, each stone the size of a fist, with a fan-shaped back and flared arms. It hovered above the floor on a suspensor field, as empty as the room.

The two halves of a broken sword lay in the seat, however. With a gasp Melaethia halted and stared at it. Caesar had no time for symbolism; he grabbed her arm.

"Come on, Melly, while our luck holds."

She came, but her face had the same stricken expression as when she had told him about killing the Pharaon. Meanwhile, the second half of the room stretched on forever. It even had a pool in it with a splashing fountain and multicolored fish. They darted in frantic formation away from Caesar's passing shadow. He was reminded of Phila, drowned somewhere beneath the palace, and a grim sense of loss caught him unexpectedly in the throat.

He tightened his grip on the blaster. Before he was through he meant to kick Salukan butt.

"The door is open," said Melaethia.

Caesar looked ahead and saw an opening in the gold paneling. He frowned and slowed his pace, approaching it cautiously. No one lurked on the other side, however, and Caesar whipped through only to find himself in yet another passageway.

"Damn!" he said, lowering his blaster. "I thought you said this went outside."

"It does," said Melaethia. "The palace guards use this entrance. It opens on the parade ground."

Caesar forced himself forward. After the airy lightness of the throne room, the unlit passageway had a narrow, claustrophobic feel that made him uneasy. He could barely see, although Melaethia seemed to have no trouble. It felt like a good place for an ambush.

Muffled sounds of battle still came from outside. Caesar tensed as they came to the exit. The confusion outside could be an advantage in their escape, or they could get caught and killed in the middle of it. He slowed, and Melaethia touched his back, making him jump.

"Yusus!" he said, trying to calm his pounding heart. "Take it easy, will you?"

"Take what?" asked Melaethia in puzzlement. "Do you—"

He shushed her quickly. Gesturing for her to stay where she was, he eased up to the exit. A slit of a skylight in the low ceiling let down a gloomy amount of illumination. The passageway widened into a sort of foyer, probably where the honor guard gathered for last-minute inspections, and the light didn't reach very far into the shadows.

Caesar looked around but saw nothing wrong. Still, he felt like a man with a live detonator counting down in his pocket. He thought about raking the shadows with blaster fire just in case, but he didn't want to waste his charge just because he was a little spooked around the edges.

His fingers closed upon the door's crossbar. For a moment he was stymied; he wasn't used to manually opened doors.

But the bar yielded to light pressure, and with a faint click the door swung open.

Outside, the crimson glare of a setting sun cast harsh shadows upon a parade ground littered with bodies. Smoke curled over a battle still waging. Without actually poking his head out as a target, Caesar saw some cover in the form of a low barrier wall running parallel to the building. It had a break by the door, but they could duck outside unseen.

He drew back to signal Melaethia, but as he did so the cold muzzle of a weapon pressed hard against the back of his neck. Caesar froze, the sour taste of fear and defeat burning his throat. Slowly, reluctantly, his mind awash with curses, he dropped his blaster and lifted his good hand in surrender.

There was a scrape as his blaster was kicked across the floor. The pressure on the back of his neck vanished.

"Turn around carefully," whispered a small, gruff voice in Saluk.

Caesar complied, trying to figure out whether he could take an armed Salukan one-handed. It probably came down to, did he want a blaster bolt between the eyes now or later? He tensed, gathering himself.

His captor, however, backed out of reach. "Don't try it." Caesar squinted, trying to see through the gloom. The Salukan wasn't big . . . a kid maybe. And maybe . . .

His heart leapt. "Phila?"

The blaster aimed at him lowered. "Caesar?"

Caesar grinned like a fool and rushed forward, but the whine of blaster fire from across the room sent him diving. He heard a choked cry from Phila and knew she was hit.

"Damned *cosquenti*!" she swore, her voice shrill with pain, and returned fire.

Scuttling across the floor on his belly with blaster bolts scorching by just above him, Caesar pulled his scattered wits back together.

"Melly!" he shouted. "Hold fire! You too, Phila! Yusus, hold fire, both of you!"

The shooting stopped, leaving the bitter stench of smoke and ion discharge in the foyer. Cautiously Caesar lifted his head.

"Phila, she's a friend."

"The hell she is," retorted Phila, gasping.

Caesar struggled to his feet. Melaethia came out of the shadows, still gripping her blaster with both hands.

"Who is this boy?" she demanded. "You can trust none of them, Caesar—"

"Phila's on our side," he said, kneeling by Phila, who was writhing on the floor. "She's just disguised as a boy. Steady, toots. Where's it hurt?"

Phila gripped him tight. "My leg. Ow!"

Caesar jerked his prodding hand away. "Sorry. It's a graze, I think. A solid hit would have slagged off everything below the knee."

She shuddered, and he put his arm around her with a comforting squeeze. He knew how much a burn hurt. But she would be okay once they got her to Beaulieu. In the meantime she was alive. He hugged her tighter.

"Thought you were dead, kid," he said thickly.

"You too," she said, muffled against his chest.

He cupped his palm against her shaven skull, feeling the tiny prickles where her hair was already growing. Amusement bubbled up inside him, pushing away the lump in his throat. He envisioned what she was going to look like with little black bristles all over her head and chuckled.

"What's funny?" demanded Phila.

Caesar sobered hastily. "Nothing. Let's get you out of here."

"Yeah," she muttered. "Good idea."

He looked up. "Give me a hand, Melly. Let's get her on her feet."

"Your arm," said Melaethia in a cold, still suspicious tone. "Don't strain it."

"I won't," he said with exasperation, "if you help. Come on."

With obvious reluctance Melaethia helped pull Phila upright. Phila bit off a cry and half collapsed against Caesar. He grabbed quickly to hold her upright, staggering a bit to keep his balance.

"Keep your weight off of it," he said. "Steady now. Get on her other side, Melly. We'll support her between us."

But Melaethia stood there. "One does not offer the hand of friendship to an enemy."

"You aren't enemies," he said irritably. "We're all on the same side."

"We have fought."

"Oh, for God's sake—" He broke off, fuming, and tried again. "Look, I told you I thought she'd drowned. We got separated down there in the water. But she's part of the team. We're all here to help you."

"Who is she?" murmured Phila to Caesar.

"Sparrow's daughter," he replied softly.

Phila stared at him a moment, then silently pulled a spare wristband from her pocket and handed it to Melaethia, who took it reluctantly.

"I want no gifts."

"It's not a gift," said Caesar, and showed her how to put it on. "It's necessary to getting out of here."

Phila tipped back her head. "Just how are we going to get out?"

He'd been wondering the same thing. "I thought you'd have some ideas."

"Mandale!" she exploded. "Don't you ever think ahead? I was going to try to steal a small airsled off the parade ground but—"

"Terrific idea," he said. "If we don't get shot out there."

"Better than getting shot in here," said Phila with a glare at Melaethia.

"Now, now," said Caesar in admonishment. "You started it. If you hadn't jumped me and scared me out of my life's growth, Melly wouldn't have had to come to my rescue."

"Yeah," said Phila, her face softening into a rueful smile. "I guess that's so."

"She is your woman?" asked Melaethia.

Caesar prayed for patience. "No," he said flatly. "She isn't. And neither are you. Now, stop stalling and lend a hand. You can resolve your cat fight later."

Slowly Melaethia came over and put her shoulder under Phila's right arm, taking most of her weight off Caesar.

"Hey," said Phila. "My feet are coming off the ground."

"Tough, shortie," said Caesar. "Let's go."

They managed a halting progress across to the door. Caesar left Melaethia supporting Phila and recovered his blaster. He eased out the door first, covering the two women as they hobbled out. In the sunlight Phila's face was a pasty hue but she wasn't complaining as they crouched behind the barrier.

The battle was over. Caesar raised himself for a better glance around, then ducked swiftly, holding his breath so that his oath strangled in his throat.

Phila gripped his knee. "What is it?"

Caesar blinked, trying to assimilate this newest problem. Dismay spread through him.

"Caesar!"

He held up a hand to shush her. The three of them huddled in a knot as a squad of troopers marched by. Caesar slid his back up the barrier until he could just peer over the top of it.

Sure enough, Kelly and 41 were prisoners. Caesar frowned, gnawing worriedly on his lip.

"They've got Kelly and 41," he said. "Damn."

Phila's black eyes met his green ones. "We have to rescue them."

He nodded. No question about that. "The only problem is how. Start thinking, toots. Melly, where are prisoners kept in this place?"

Kelly sat on the stone floor of a featureless cell containing neither window, door, nor ceiling. The walls rose in a smooth cylinder to about three meters, then were topped by a metal railing. A gaunt Salukan in the dark green uniform of DUR, a mailord's rank upon his sleeve and the Star of Pharaon hanging at his throat, looked down at Kelly with an expression of smug satisfaction.

So far he had made no attempt to talk to Kelly. He simply stared and smiled.

Kelly glared back. "Where is my operative? How long are you going to keep him in interrogation?"

The mailord did not reply. In frustration Kelly maneuvered himself stiffly to his feet and slowly paced around the cell. He still felt wobbly and knew he should conserve his strength, but he was too worried about 41.

They'd been ready to fight as soon as they made a forced landing, but troopers had swarmed the craft, giving them no real chance. A battle had been fought at the palace, but it was mostly over by the time Kelly and 41 were captured. They saw disarmed troopers being marched into barracks by other troopers, but no one explained what was going on.

At the moment Kelly didn't care. He kept thinking about the mind sieve with an uncontrollable clutch of fear in his gut. It was worse than torture. It robbed a man of a little piece of his soul. For the rest of his life Kelly would have nightmares of his session in that metal chair. He didn't want to go through it again, risking madness or death or both.

As for 41, he'd been taken away immediately by guards. And they were still in the Defended City. Kelly expected transfer to Godinye Prison at any minute. Sometime during that transfer he would have to make a break for freedom or die in the attempt. He wasn't going to spend the next several years rotting in Godinye's torture chambers, kept alive by chemicals while all the security blocks in his mind were deconditioned and broken down.

An infuriating wave of shakiness passed through him. Kelly sat down again and leaned his head against the wall. When the drug wore off he wouldn't be able to do much at all. He hoped his chance came before then.

Glancing up at the mailord, he tried again: "At least tell me if my friend is being held in a separate cell or if he is—"

"Is this the other Earther?" asked a rich, arrogant voice.

The Salukan who joined the mailord had to be a courtier. He wore armor decorated with bands of gold and silver with a linen cloak of white falling from his shoulders. His bronze skin gleamed with oil and his razor-thin features had a cruel, rapacious cast to them that warned Kelly he would be no ally.

The mailord inclined profoundly. "Yes, Vaudan. He is Commander Bryan Kelly of AIA Special Operations."

"Ah," said the vaudan while Kelly got to his feet in astonishment at being identified so quickly. "The Space Hawks." Leaning over the railing, the vaudan spread his hand in a mock gesture of welcome. "Your reputation precedes you, Commander. I admire your prowess in penetrating our security all the way inside the Defended City. You are too late, however, to assassinate Nefir. He is dead."

Kelly digested this information with a blink. Assassination was a way of life for most of the upper-class Salukan population throughout the Empire, but pharaons usually died of extreme old age.

"Too bad," he said casually.

The vaudan smiled. "But then, that was not your mission, was it? You have come for a different, much less spectacular purpose. An old man named Arnaht . . ."

He went on, but Kelly ceased to hear what he was saying. Who was the leak? he wondered furiously. Rafael? One of Sparrow's children? Sparrow himself?

Either that, or they had already cracked open 41.

Kelly fought off the sick feeling of defeat and looked up at the vaudan with a shrug. He wasn't going to give them the satisfaction of gloating.

"A minor informer of no specific importance," he said.

The vaudan frowned. "Wrong! You came here to help him defect. You intended to—"

"Defect?" Kelly forced a scornful laugh. "Why would we carry out a suicide mission to infiltrate Byiul for one old man who's been sending us fake information supplied by DUR for years?"

It was a bluff, calculated on the chance that Sparrow had been a double agent, and Kelly saw it strike home. The vaudan drew back in visible anger.

"Mailord Cocipec! You were supposed to have a full briefing on this matter. Have you bungled yet again?"

The mailord inclined hastily. "No, Vaudan. I—"

"Nefir showed you too much patience. DUR has become a useless entity, feeding on its own fat and accomplishing nothing."

"Excellency," said Cocipec. "We have already broken the

traitor Rafael and are at this very moment rounding up his network of informants. If I may transfer these Earthers to my interrogation facilities at Godinye, I assure you that they—''

''No,'' said the vaudan curtly. He gestured at another figure whom Kelly could not see except for a glimpse of a tan-colored uniform. ''Mailord Huvfit will now take charge of interrogation.''

''The military!'' Cocipec sneered. ''They are years out of date. They won't—''

''My decision is spoken!'' snapped the vaudan.

Cocipec inclined, looking as though he had strangled. Huvfit moved closer to the railing. His imperial sash glittered as he turned.

''Things are changing in Byiul for the better,'' he said in a pompous, self-important voice. ''Nefir allowed the military and the fleet to go begging while he indulged in foolish projects. DUR was his pet, but as our new Pharaon, Raumses will make many changes.''

''Excellency,'' said Cocipec in quiet desperation. ''I plead once again to be allowed to remain upon this case. I have been with it from the first. It was I who suspected Earthers instead of insurrectionists. I promise you—''

Huvfit laughed. ''Ahe! Beg, Cocipec. Beg for your position. Soon you may be begging for your head.''

Cocipec took a step back. ''And what will you do with these men? Whip them until they talk? They're specialists, trained and conditioned to resist all but the most sophisticated methods. You haven't even an adequate verifier scan.''

''Coward!'' roared Huvfit. ''You are squirming in your eagerness to get out of here. You will seize any excuse, but we all know your loyalty was to Nefir, not Raumses. You want to hole up in that fortress of yours across the canal and start a counter-rebellion. But it isn't going to happen. Arrest him.''

''No—''

Guards hustled Cocipec away. Huvfit and Raumses stared down at Kelly once again.

''An interesting subject,'' said Raumses. ''I look forward to your findings, Mailord.''

Raumses walked away with a swirl of his white cloak. Huvfit smiled down at Kelly.

"A Space Hawk, eh? Well, you're no better than any other weak-minded Earther. We'll soon have you telling us everything we want to know."

Kelly made no answer, but he had the sick suspicion that perhaps Huvfit was right.

On Street 119r, Beaulieu stretched out her legs cautiously. They were going to sleep curled up in this hiding place. She'd been here an hour, crouched on a rooftop overlooking the street. 41 and Kelly should have joined her by now. And Arnaht would be arriving within the next five minutes, if he was coming at all.

So far she had seen no evidence of a trap. That puzzled her because she agreed entirely with 41's assessment of the situation.

Perhaps there wasn't going to be a trap laid here because 41, Kelly, and even Arnaht had all been arrested. Perhaps she was the only one left.

Beaulieu frowned, not liking that thought at all. She felt a moment of panic and wondered what she was doing out here on an alien planet deep in enemy territory instead of lecturing on anatomy at the University of Science. Some kind of attempt to cling to her vanished youth—at least that's what she'd been accused of when she first joined the Space Hawks several months ago. She'd always told herself it wasn't that. She was wasted as a teacher. She was too impatient. She wanted to be out in the galaxy achieving things, making a difference.

Bringing a man to freedom seemed like a good way of making a difference when Kelly first told them about this mission. Now, crouched on a rooftop in the blasting heat of late afternoon with time running out and everyone in the squad either presumed dead or missing, she saw the futility of it all.

Her eyes ached and burned, but she'd learned not to cry in medical school. "Grief is a normal, natural reaction that should be expressed," said her psychology trainer. But she didn't want to grieve. That would mean giving up hope for the others.

What had happened to 41 and Kelly? If any two could get out of a tight spot, they could. She admired Kelly. Despite his relative youth and privileged background as the son of an admiral and Earth's Minister of Culture, he was a good leader—by turns tough and compassionate—who genuinely cared for his squad and had an incisive grasp of military strategy.

She didn't know about 41 yet. Kelly's faith in him tended to color her thinking. She'd tried kindness, criticism, and camaraderie. Sometimes 41 responded; sometimes he did not. One approach seemed to work no better than the others. And she was left with no clear conclusions except the obvious: he was a fierce, self-protective creature who'd been seriously abused as a child, who fitted in nowhere, had no culture which claimed him, had no family to give him a stable foundation, and therefore had no basis for giving anyone his loyalty.

What if he turned on Kelly and gave him to the Salukan authorities? What if he decided he wanted to be a Salukan now instead of a human?

That's what the analysts at AIA HQ thought would happen. But so far 41 was doing his job. He had completed the rendezvous with Sparrow when Kelly failed to turn up. He came back to her in the warehouse to report. Both times he could have abandoned the squad. He could have ignored Kelly's call for help.

"He may be the soundest one of us all," she muttered aloud.

Sitting here thinking and sweating and worrying wasn't accomplishing anything. She checked her chron. Just over an hour until check-in with Siggerson. They hadn't much time to get beyond the city perimeter.

She felt a fresh cramp of worry. She couldn't wait here much longer for people who weren't going to show up. Did she write them off and get herself to safety? Did she go back in search of them?

Where? Where would she search? Where would she start in a city of 18 million inhabitants?

And how would she forgive herself, flying home on the *Valiant* with Siggerson while the others were left behind?

"Damn!"

She pulled her feet under her and started down the outside steps leading from the rooftop to the street. A scrawny child with a dirty hairlock and a shaved head scarred from vermin bites stared at her. She glared at him, and he ran.

She would go to the empty house where they had stashed the big equipment and she would get the scanner. She ought to be able to calibrate it to locate all of them by their wristbands.

They're dead; you're being irrational.

Beaulieu pushed the thought away.

At the same time, she spotted Arnaht coming toward her on the street. He stumbled along, glancing over his shoulder, glancing suspiciously at every face, his pace unsteady. He wore tailored, nondescript clothes and had drawn a hood over his head to shield himself from the sun. He carried a small package beneath his arm and clutched it as though he believed someone might steal it at any moment.

The way he looked and acted, probably a dozen citizens had reported him as a suspicious character.

Beaulieu curbed exasperation and strode toward him.

"Sparrow!" she said, causing him to start and veer away from her before he halted, panting a little, his eyes burning with madness or anger or grief.

"Out of my path, *vasweem*," he said gruffly, the insult sounding strange on his cultured tongue. "I am late and have no time for—"

She gripped his arm. "I'm with Peregrine," she said.

He stared at her, his mouth working. She frowned, noting signs of shock, and tightened her grip on his arm.

"Have you been followed?"

"No." He blinked rapidly several times, and she longed for her medikit. "At least, I don't think so. I lost the monitor sometime ago. And I told the others the wrong location."

A chill ran down Beaulieu's spine. "Others?" she said sharply. "The DUR?"

"Hush!" he said in alarm, glancing around. "Let no one hear."

"Let's keep walking." To her relief he came with her. "How did DUR find out?"

He made a little noise of despair. "They caught me . . . sometime ago. I have been serving them, taking false messages to be sent to you. But I didn't! I mean, I substituted accurate information whenever possible. This—" He tapped the package beneath his arm. "This is very important. My gift to your people."

He stopped walking. "I can't go!" he said wildly. "I can't leave them!"

His behavior was attracting notice. Beaulieu gave him a quick shake. "Keep walking!" she said. "Who can't you leave? Your family? They wouldn't come?"

He sighed, his face so bleak and old she felt sympathy in spite of herself. But this wasn't the time or the place to offer comfort. She kept him walking, conscious of dwindling time.

It was a long, hot, dusty walk to the Sang Quarter. Beaulieu's imagination had her expecting a contingent of troopers waiting for them, but the squalid, half-abandoned residential area was quiescent except for a handful of children shrieking in play. They were chasing a starved-looking animal that cowered and cringed and darted frantically to escape their sticks.

Beaulieu's temper nearly got the better of her judgment, and just in time she stopped herself from grabbing a stick and beating the nearest child. Their laughter and cruelty sickened her. She was conscious suddenly of the strangeness of this place. All day she had observed Salukans, seeking points of similarity in their culture with her own. Now she felt just how alien they were. Not that cruelty was confined strictly to them. Humans were renowned for their own violent tendencies.

But combined with the heat and the smells of squalor mixed with exotic spices and the peculiar architecture was the savagery always pushing against its veneer of civilization. A savagery quite different from the human kind.

She wanted desperately to leave, to be back among her own kind. She wanted to breathe controlled-temperature air. She wanted to hear Glish spoken around her. She wanted to walk down a corridor on a space station, mingling with a dozen or so races, species, and cultures without having to fear spy monitors or sudden knife thrusts from nowhere. She wanted to see faces that weren't closed with paranoia.

She wanted to go home.

The house where they had stashed the grav-flats and coolers had been raided—by children, from the looks of how everything had been scattered. Beaulieu, longing for a drink, stared at the empty cooler in dismay. The grav-flat was gone, stolen and stripped for parts, no doubt. She found two environmental suits; one was intact and looked operational, but the other was missing its helmet and gloves. The rest were gone entirely.

Beaulieu kicked through the trash and swore aloud. Arnaht walked out to the house's ruined courtyard and seated himself on a fallen section of the wall. His dejected figure brought Beaulieu out of her anger. She recalled her grandiose speech to 41 earlier that day about saving Arnaht to make all of this mean something.

Well, now that her own words had been flung back in her face, she found them pretty bitter. The others, for whatever reason, weren't going to make it. Her own duty was plain.

Tucking the one environmental suit under her arm, she walked out into the courtyard.

"Come," she said. "We have to go beyond the city perimeters to make contact with our ship."

He rose obediently to his feet. "When will the others come?"

"I don't know," she said grimly, leading him to the break in the wall, through it, and down into the dry drainage ditch. Ahead of them stretched the forbidding Valu Desert as bleak and empty now as it had been when they came. She forced herself to smile at the old man. "Our job is to get in position for pick-up."

Arnaht stopped and looked back. "Here," he said, thrusting the package into her hands. "Take this. It is all that is really important."

"Wait," said Beaulieu in startlement. "What are you—"

"All that I am is here. My children, the bones of my wife."

She grabbed his arm. "You can't go back. It won't help your children. And you'll be arrested."

His weary, grieving eyes met hers. "The package contains a treasure trove of classified data. You have people who can decode it. I am not needed."

"Yes, you are!" she said so vehemently he blinked. "We came to get you out. You deserve freedom after seventeen years of risking your life to help us."

The light in his eyes faded. "I am too old."

"Old or not, you aren't staying! It won't help anyone."

He shook free of her hand. "Why should you care? You want to parade me around the Alliance like a tame huns-muth in a zoo. An exhibit to illustrate the fact that some Salukans aren't such bad fellows."

He was showing natural remorse, an expected reaction to his decision to leave everything he knew behind. But right now she could care less about how he felt or what he wanted.

"Damn you! Four people have died to get you out. You're coming, and I don't care what the hell you do in the Alliance. You can go sit in a cave on a colony world. But you are leaving Gamael, and you're going to do it now."

He stared at her coldly. "What will you do to force me? Draw your weapon? Shoot me?"

That had been in Beaulieu's mind. Hastily she squelched it.

Arnaht spread his hands. "I have given enough! I risked my life, alienated my children, shamed the honor of my wife. No more!"

He turned and hurried away from her. Beaulieu watched him a moment, then hefted the package in her hands. She aimed and threw it so that it hit him in the back. He stumbled and turned in surprise, staring first at her, then at the package lying on the ground at his feet.

"Fool!" he said angrily. "You must take it. Important data is—"

"Maybe it's a bomb. I think you betrayed us to the DUR. And that package is meant to finish us off by blowing up our ship. No deal, Arnaht. If you don't come, the package doesn't either."

He picked it up, carefully brushing off the dust. She could not read his expression at all.

"It is not a bomb," he said at last. "My word—"

"Sorry," she said harshly. "I don't know what a Salukan's word is good for."

He stiffened and reached for his side, but he did not carry a dagger. The instinctive action seemed to embarrass him, for the anger faded from his face and he made a little gesture of resignation.

"It's Melaethia," he said. "She has been taken into the Pharaon's Court of Women. Dausal, my son, was lost to me from the day he became a cadet. If he is permitted to live for his betrayal of me to the authorities, he will probably succeed in his career. But Melaethia trapped in the Defended City, hemmed in like a slave with ritual, forced to think of nothing but the pleasure and capricious whim of that tyrant—"

His voice broke and he bent over, making a harsh gasping noise. Beaulieu rushed to him, thinking he was having an attack, but it was only the Salukan way of grief. Her own anger faded. She put a comforting hand upon his shoulder.

"Come," she said quietly. "Going back won't save her now. If Kelly were here, he might think of a way to get her out. But he—he isn't." She swallowed hard. "I'm sure Melaethia knows how much you love her. Come."

Slowly, broken in spirit again, he came with her into the desert, where the bruised, bleary eye of the sun sank into the horizon and desolation howled with the wind.

12

Earthers are a pestilent species, hard to kill, impossible to frighten.

—Nomarch Tuc, following the Battle of Gadrant Nebula

Years before, when he'd gone to his first pleasure planet with the mercenaries he belonged to, 41 had watched a cheaply produced long-vid involving all sorts of improbable adventures and tortures. In it, weapons never ran out of plasma charge or ammunition, the characters were able to go for days without rest or food, and the heroine fainted in the agony booth and was spared feeling any of the pain.

Suspended by his shackled wrists in a wet interrogation cell, 41 wished it were possible to really pass out from pain. But no matter how bad it got, every agonizing sensation transmitted straight to his brain, and he had no blood loss or injury serious enough to grant him unconsciousness.

Kelly, on the other hand, was out cold and had been for a long time. Periodically one of the guards grabbed him by the hair and gave him a jerk, but he had not roused. He was lucky.

Cold water sluiced over 41 in a deluge, making him gasp. He tensed, knowing what would follow. Within seconds the charged whips cracked—one, two—upon him from opposite sides. One split across his blaster burn and he cried out, almost oblivious to the electrical shock jerking him as the whips curled away.

The cell blurred into a sickly yellow. There was still blood in his eyes from a previous cut on his forehead. He closed his eyes, gasping for every shallow, constricted breath. His hide felt raw, blistered, and abraded. He wanted to be sick, but his stomach had long since emptied, and a bout of dry heaves left him hanging weak and exhausted.

''Enough,'' said a voice from the darkness.

The sound of running water cut off. The guards coiled their whips and stepped back. 41 rubbed his face upon his arm. His face was wet, from water, tears, or blood, he could not tell.

The minlord supervising his torture stood before him, hands clasped at his back, eyes flat and merciless as they studied 41.

''You have Salukan blood in your veins,'' he said.

He ran a finger across 41's burned chest, and 41 shuddered in anguish. He would have kicked the minlord, but his feet were tied down. 41 glared blearily at him, imagining the pleasure of disemboweling him with a dirty knife.

The minlord held up his finger and it was smeared with 41's amber blood. ''Tell me,'' he said, sounding almost friendly. ''Why do you serve an Earther? You have no reason to be with them at all.''

Slowly 41 lifted his head to meet the minlord's eyes. ''I am human,'' he said hoarsely.

''*Suh*, where is it in you? In the southern hemisphere there are pale ones—pale hair, pale skin, no cheek ridges. Our medics can run a full anatomical check on you and determine your breeding.''

For a moment 41 felt the tug of curiosity and temptation. Then he drew back in anger. He spat, nearly hitting the minlord in the face with his spittle.

''I know my breeding. And I know the way of a Salukan lie. Use your mind-twisting upon someone else. It won't work on me.''

The minlord frowned; obviously he had not expected his

mental touch to be detected. "Interesting," he mused, pacing back and forth in front of 41. "You felt my touch. That indicates latent abilities of your own. Very rare in most bloodlines. Even rarer in crossbreeds."

Unbidden, a memory of the Old Ones flashed through 41's mind. They had taught him much in the way of self-protection—including telepathic protection—when he was a young child. He longed to live within that time again, to know no hurt, no distrust, no grief.

He closed his eyes, feeling the heavy drag of exhaustion, but the minlord gripped his jaw and shook him.

"Even more reason to side with us. You could be trained to use—"

"I am not a dog. I do not need your training."

The minlord's claws dug into 41's skin before he released him. "So much distrust. Join us. Torture is for Earthers, not Salukans. Speak to us freely and a place can be found for you within the—"

"No!"

"You look like us. You belong with us. How many Earthers treat you as an equal? Are you not regarded with suspicion wherever you go?"

That was true. 41 frowned. "The Earthers allow me life," he said at last. "Here I am an abomination."

The minlord laughed. "That old superstition. Among the uneducated on the fringes of the Empire, perhaps. Here on Gamael, we are much more civilized."

"You lie," said 41.

The minlord's amusement faded. He stepped back. "Fool," he said in contempt. "You could have your life, but if you choose to die with this Earther, so be it." He gestured at the guards. "Send for an escort. We'll transfer them down to Level 3. They should be weakened enough for the mind sieve to work now."

He started out, then glanced back. "You have a short time to reflect on your choice. Think wisely."

They walked out, leaving 41 hanging there in darkness and pain.

Kelly, who'd regained consciousness during their conversation but played possum, waited until the door slammed shut, then he lifted his head and tried to see through the gloom. 41 remained a vague shape, not really seen.

"The minlord had a point," he said softly.

41 jerked his shackles in startlement. "How long have you been awake?"

"Long enough." Kelly waited a moment but his curiosity was too strong to ignore. "Why didn't you take his offer?"

"Trust a Salukan?" retorted 41 with scorn. He spat. "I'd be dead in a week, or else sentenced to hard labor. I know their ways."

Kelly frowned. "A week of life would be more than you've got right now. You might even be able to escape. Why not take the chance?"

"I do not understand," said 41 stiffly. "Is this another test of my loyalty? Do you wish me to change sides?"

"It's the expedient thing to do, isn't it?"

"Would you?"

"No," said Kelly. "I would not. Not at any cost."

"Why not?"

Kelly smiled briefly to himself, not minding if 41 turned the tables on their conversation. "Because of who I am, who my parents are, and how I was raised."

"That is no answer."

"No, it's not," agreed Kelly. "I followed that kind of glib patriotism all the way through the Academy. When I got my first ship assignment, however, I found I had to think for myself and make some decisions. The court-martial clinched it. When I was acquitted of all charges, I found I couldn't go back to that mindless devotion to duty required of military personnel. I couldn't just follow orders without question."

"An admiral's son on trial?" said 41 in disbelief.

"Personal privilege isn't recognized as a defense against mutiny charges," said Kelly. "I have my own career just as my father, mother, older brother, and sisters have theirs. We each stand on our own."

"Mutiny," said 41.

"Yes. I'll tell you about it someday," said Kelly. "I considered a few civilian jobs and decided I couldn't bear to be planetbound, pushing paper, and making no difference."

"So you became a Space Hawk to make a difference."

41 sounded ironical. Kelly sighed. He probably couldn't make 41 understand without sounding corny and foolish, but he wanted to try. Honesty on his side might lead to honesty from 41.

"When I was very young, seven years old, we lived on a planet in the Killian System. My mother was serving there as Earth's ambassadress; my father was away in service. I had a nanny from the native population. Basha took excellent care of me. At the time she was my best friend.

"One day we came home from an outing just as a small Salukan force broke through planetary defenses and attacked the capital. Basha threw me down and shielded me from the strafing with her body. Then we made our way inside the embassy. She had saved my life, but when the embassy staff was evacuated, Basha wasn't allowed to come with us to safety. I pleaded on her behalf, but no one listened.

"We left Killian, never to return. Later, after several years of occupation, the Salukans were driven out. I tried to locate Basha, but never found her."

Kelly clenched his fists, feeling the answering cramp in his wrists. "Maybe she's still alive. Maybe she died during the occupation. I'll never know. But I grew up ashamed of that day."

"Why? It was an act of adults. Children have no power."

"True." Kelly wiped his sweating face on his arm while he sought words. "But children know a dishonorable act when they see it. I know now that the embassy had no choice really. They couldn't take everyone; the selection process would have been agonizing. But I owed Basha my life; for the first time I learned about obligations. I vowed that when I was an adult I would work to stop oppression—in any form, not just Salukan conquest."

41 stirred and loosed a soft groan. "There will be no more missions for us."

"No, but we didn't fail," said Kelly. He hesitated, then added, "Thanks for coming back for me."

"I could do nothing else," said 41.

Silence stretched between them while Kelly digested that answer. For gruff, undemonstrative 41, it was the closest to an open declaration of firm friendship he could make. Warmed, Kelly smiled at him.

"Nevertheless," said Kelly, "thank you."

"You asked me why I refused the minlord," said 41 finally. 'What you will not do, I will not do. It is how I learn the ways of humans. I *want* to be human, Kelly. I want to be like . . ."

His voice trailed off and he said no more.

"Well," said Kelly gently, "I'm not sure you picked the best role model in the galaxy. I'm not perfect."

"No human is," retorted 41.

Kelly laughed, wringing a sharp twinge from his wound that made him gasp, but his laughter went on just the same. After a moment 41 joined him.

The lights snapped on. In came the guards.

"Interesting that you find interrogation so amusing," said the minlord harshly.

Kelly shrugged as far as his shackles would allow. "A human trait, I'm afraid."

He glanced at 41 as he spoke, and saw 41's eyes gleam in appreciation.

"Soon you will be screaming," said the minlord, and gestured. "Take them to the mind sieve."

The guards released Kelly's feet, then his arms, lowering him so roughly he staggered and nearly lost his balance. He doubled over, clutching his stomach, and managed to straighten in time to avoid being struck. He measured the odds while 41 was being released. Two against five armed men. Pretty poor odds.

41 sagged to the ground. Both of his guards bent over to hoist him up, and he seized one by the chest, slamming him into the other.

Kelly took advantage of the distraction to round on his nearest guard. The man, however, was expecting him to try it and whipped out his blaster. Kelly kicked it from his hand, although the effort pulled at his bandage and sent a wave of dizziness through him. He staggered, trying not to fall down, and that saved him from the other guard's grab.

Sensing the guard looming over him, Kelly twisted desperately with a rabbit punch to his abdomen. It was a good thing the punch was weak because he'd forgotten the Salukans had a cartilage plate there. A harder blow would have broken his knuckles. Gasping, Kelly swung again, but he'd lost his moment of advantage. Both guards grabbed him and pulled him upright. One held him and the other struck him with a hammer blow right over the heart.

Pain exploded through Kelly's chest, a pain so immense and unbelievable he was filled with admiration. The guard hit him again. Thunder in his ears, in his chest. As he fell, he felt his heart stop . . .

He awakened moments later, groggy and gagging down bubbles of air, to find himself being dragged down a corridor with his toes scraping and bumping the ground. His head weighed a ton. With dizzying effort he lifted it.

The walls had a dismaying tendency to melt together ahead of them. Kelly blinked, trying to clear his mind of the desire to go back to sleep. He wasn't going through the mind sieve ever again.

The walls were still stuck together. No. Kelly squinted and concentrated very hard. They were approaching the end of the corridor. A lift waited there. He held himself together, ignoring the dull agony in his chest, and chose his moment.

Just before the guards slowed to a halt, Kelly picked up his feet and found purchase on the floor. He surged forward, pushing the guards' own impetus to catch them off balance. They staggered, grunting in surprise, but by then they were slamming into the wall.

Kelly yanked his arm free and snatched a dagger. He stabbed its owner and whirled in time to duck under the other guard's attack. Kelly slashed him with the dagger and got his blaster.

Hasty blaster fire from 41's guards missed Kelly by a hair. Giving swift thanks for the weapons' notorious inaccuracy, Kelly fired back. Breathless, blinking back little black dots dancing in front of his eyes, Kelly's aim wasn't much better, and for a moment he feared he'd shot 41.

The minlord came at a run. *"Hut, avi! Aret chese!"*

He fired at the same time as the remaining guard. Kelly threw himself flat, knowing he was done for now. But neither hit him.

He heard a scream, and a blaster bolt went wide, hitting the ceiling. The minlord and guard crumpled, leaving 41 collapsing to his knees. Behind him, Kelly saw three figures coming along the corridor. Three weaving, fuzzy figures with haloes of light shining behind them from the ceiling light.

"Boss?" said one.

Kelly frowned, trying to cling to the skeetering edges of consciousness. One of the three fired at the ceiling, putting the surveillance cams out of commission. Another ran forward, pausing briefly to set a hand on 41's shoulder, then coming to Kelly. A man colored dark blue with yellow tattoos on his cheeks and a thatch of hair with streaks of dye missing to show irrepressible red.

"Hey, boss," he said in Glish, kneeling beside Kelly to grip him by the shoulder. "You okay? You look like hell."

Kelly grinned, relief spreading through him like a healing salve. "Caesar," he whispered hoarsely. "You are the ugliest, most god-awful sight for sore eyes I've ever seen. Thank God you came."

"Well, sure," said Caesar, grinning broadly. "You didn't think I'd ditch you guys, did you? We Hawks got to flock together, right?"

Kelly groaned because it hurt too much to laugh. Caesar's jokes were as bad as ever. "I should have known you wouldn't drown."

"Damned near did." Caesar's grin faded and he glanced over his shoulder. "We better get out of here. Can you stand? It's up to you to walk because no one can carry you. We're all in pretty bad shape."

Kelly lifted his head and slowly counted. Including Caesar and himself, there were five. At least there were once he stopped seeing double.

"Full squad complement." He frowned and looked again. "That's not Beaulieu."

"Nope." Caesar looked suddenly concerned. "Hey, where is she? Yusus, I don't think I'm up to another rescue."

"You didn't rescue us," said 41 with a ghost of his old prickliness. "We were . . . escaping . . . when you came."

"Now, look," began Caesar.

"Save it," said Kelly wearily. "Both of you. We've got to find her—"

"No," said 41. He started to get to his feet but didn't quite make it. "She's with . . . Sparrow."

Kelly's attention sharpened. He glanced at Caesar and held out his hand. "Help me up."

Caesar complied, grunting a little with the effort. Kelly noticed then that he was only using one arm. And Phila was leaning on a battered Salukan woman. Kelly frowned at Caesar.

"This is not time to be collecting girlfriends—"

"Whoa, boss. Whoa!" said Caesar indignantly. "She's Sparrow's kid. Mel, this is Kelly and that's 41."

The young woman, who beneath her bruises had a certain grace and beauty in the Salukan fashion, inclined slightly. "I thank all of you for your assistance to my father . . . and myself." She hesitated, then added, "My proper name is Melaethia."

Kelly smiled at her, but he was too tired for amentities. "You're right, Caesar, We'd better get out of here. We came in an aircab. If we can steal a craft, we'll be in the desert before—"

41 was shaking his head. Caesar glanced at his chron and let out a sharp exclamation.

"What is it?" said Kelly. He looked at his own chron and felt deflated as though all the air had been driven anew from his lungs.

They'd run out of time.

13

Draw into yourself and hear the beating of your own heart. Feel the blood coursing through your veins. That is your courage. As long as your heart beats and your blood flows, you cannot fail.

—from the *Warrior Code*

All heart seemed to sag out of the group. Kelly weaved over to a wall and leaned against it.

"We aren't finished yet," he said. "We've got a backup time—"

"Aw, yusus, boss," said Caesar in disgust. "Do you really think Siggie can keep out of sight that long? He'll pick up Sparrow and Beaulieu and head for home."

Kelly glared at him. "Belay that, Samms. Siggerson will carry out his orders to the full extent of his ability. Our job is to find a way out of here."

Caesar stiffened under the reprimand. Phila pulled away from Melaethia's support and hopped forward.

"It'll be tough stealing a craft," she said. "After all the fighting, the survivors will be edgy and alert. Caesar, do you have any explosives left?"

"Nope. I'm fresh out."

Kelly frowned. He rubbed his chest, wincing, and pushed himself away from the wall to kneel beside 41, who had not yet gotten off the floor.

"We haven't much time before this minlord and his men

are missed,'' he said quietly to 41, wondering how much 41 had left to give. ''We need an aircraft that will hold everyone yet be fast. Once we're airborne we've got to outrun the trackers.''

41 rubbed his eyes before meeting Kelly's gaze. ''Agreed,'' he said with a sigh. ''But I keep falling down.''

Kelly grasped his shoulder and gave him a worried smile, aware that 41 needed medical attention as much as or more than he did himself but that they weren't going to get any for a long while.

Getting to his feet, Kelly turned to Phila. ''Everything accomplished?'' he asked, referring to her job of planting snoops throughout the palace.

She nodded. ''Yes, sir.''

''Good.'' He glanced around at them, making his decisions. ''41, you and Melaethia change into these uniforms. The rest of us will be your prisoners whom you're transporting to Godinye. That gives us a reason to be out there.''

Melaethia looked startled and pulled Caesar aside to speak to him in a low, rapid voice. 41 met Kelly's gaze and bared his teeth in approval. He crawled over to the nearest guard and unfastened his tunic.

Kelly glanced at the scanners overhead. ''Phila, how long will these things be out?''

She looked worriedly at them. ''Hard to estimate. If mop-up operations have commenced, they may notice the circuits have been blown along here and power them up again. On the other hand, if they're busy enough, we could have all the time we need.''

Not with the vaudan impatient for the results of their interrogation, thought Kelly. But he didn't voice that doubt aloud.

''Commander,'' said Caesar rather formally.

Kelly turned. Caesar still stood by Melaethia, who was shaking her hands vehemently. Kelly went over to them.

''Boss,'' said Caesar quietly. ''Using a civie for—''

Kelly glanced at Melaethia. She was his height, perhaps a couple of centimeters taller. Her eyes flicked nervously past him to the others and to 41, now half dressed in an imperial uniform.

"See," said Caesar, inching closer to Kelly so the others couldn't hear. "She's been in the harem. No one's even supposed to see her face. She—"

Impatience flared inside Kelly. He frowned at Melaethia. "You're the daughter of Arnaht? Do you want to be with him or not?"

"Yes," she whispered.

"Boss—"

Kelly held up his hand. "Look, I'm sorry we don't have time for you to get used to us. We're strange. We're Earthers. I know that. But to get out of here, to get to your father, we need to use every advantage we've got. You can help us by disguising yourself as a guard."

"I understand," said Melaethia in agitation. "But no matter what guise I wear, the real guards will smell me. I—" She broke off in visible embarrassment and looked at Caesar for help.

"She's pregnant," said Caesar, clearing his throat. "Uh, by the Pharaon."

Kelly gazed into Caesar's green eyes, then looked back at the girl. "I see," he said slowly, blinking over the implications. "All right. But she still can't go outside looking like an escapee from the harem. I'll be the guard, but she'd still better put on the minlord's clothes."

"Right," said Caesar, taking Melaethia's arm.

"But it will not—"

"Maybe no one will notice." Caesar gave her an encouraging smile. "Go ahead."

Still looking doubtful, she knelt to gingerly remove the minlord's clothes and wig. Caesar glanced at 41, then grasped Kelly's arm.

"Boss, you look like hell. I don't think you and 41 can walk that far, much less—"

"We've got one chance," said Kelly, gritting his teeth against the need to sit down. He couldn't afford to go shocky now. "Give me some help."

With a worried nod, Caesar complied.

Minutes later they were ready. Breathless, wishing he had

a stiff shot of Rymian gin as a painkiller, Kelly glanced around at them all.

"Just keep remembering that we're alive," he said. "We've made it this far. We'll make it to the end. We *can* do it."

They nodded—hurting, tired, and ready to follow him anywhere.

Kelly drew in a determined breath. "Let's go, people."

As soon as the sun set, temperatures fell rapidly in the Valu Desert. Beaulieu shivered as she gazed across the empty expanse. A wash of amber lingered above the horizon. The air felt heavy upon her skin. No wind blew, and neither animal nor insect stirred the silence. The bleached whiteness of the ground reflected back the darkening hues of twilight.

Behind her the lights of Byiul shimmered like jewels upon the velvet backdrop of the mountains. The perimeters would be closing, sealing the inhabitants inside.

There was an unaccustomed burning in the back of Beaulieu's throat, and tears stung her eyes. "Goodbye, my friends," she whispered in the old Earth dialect passed down generation after generation in her family.

Swallowing hard, she glanced at Arnaht, who stared across the infinite desert emptiness, and handed him a wristband.

"Put this on," she said.

She helped him fasten it and glanced back once more. No one. It was as though that last look back killed all the disappointment within her. She could not let herself go on hoping the others would make it. It was time to call the *Valiant*.

She flicked the setting on her comm to the *Valiant*'s specialized frequency, scrambled. "Beaulieu to *Valiant*. Come in, please. Beaulieu to *Valiant*."

She waited a moment with Arnaht standing apart from her. The hiss of silence on the comm tightened her nerves. She felt a coldness that had nothing to do with the falling temperature.

"*Valiant* responding," came Siggerson's voice through a spit of scrambler static. "Ready for pickup."

Her heart seemed to lift into her throat. She swallowed,

but her voice was not steady as she replied, "Acknowledged. Commence pickup."

The disorienting sensation of teleport blurred everything around her. When things cleared, she found herself standing on the teleport platform. Siggerson's gaunt face was stretched in what came close to a smile. It faded, however, as he realized no one else was coming up with them.

He glanced at his board and tapped a control with a frown. "I don't understand. This shows no incoming materializations. Where are the rest?"

Beaulieu stepped off the platform and wearily unfastened her wristband to store it. "We're it, I'm afraid. Kelly and 41 got caught, I think, and—"

"Think!" Siggerson glared at her. "Don't you know?"

"No. We were separated," she said, equally angry. "I don't have to justify my actions to you. I followed orders and brought Sparrow here."

Siggerson glanced past her to the Salukan, who was gazing around the small teleport bay with undisguised awe. "What's in that box?"

Arnaht apparently understood some Glish, for he shot Siggerson a swift, apprehensive look and hugged the package tighter to his chest.

"Data," said Beaulieu for him.

Siggerson rose to his feet. "Hand it over. I have to run it through a scan-check."

Arnaht drew back. "Erasure," he said in Saluk, staring at Beaulieu in appeal.

"He's afraid you'll erase—"

"Nonsense!" snapped Siggerson. "Data cohesion isn't that fragile. Come on. Hand it over."

Beaulieu glanced at Arnaht. "He'll be careful," she said in Saluk. "It's standard procedure. You can't bring unauthorized containers aboard without being checked. And while Siggerson runs a scan on your package, I'll need to give you a checkup in my lab. There are certain bacteria which might—"

The door to the teleport room opened automatically for her, and she found her path blocked in the corridor by a creature all sleek shadings of smoke and silver. It crouched with its long, luxuriant tail wrapped neatly around its paws.

It chittered impatiently, gazing up at her with round, intelligent blue eyes.

Sentient and highly independent, Ouoji had turned out to be female, much to Siggerson's disappointment. He also picked out a Scandinavian name for her, which she rejected with much tail lashing and anger. But once all that was settled, she had proven to be an affectionate creature and was usually found on the flight deck, sitting on the edge of Siggerson's control board.

Beaulieu always felt slightly ridiculous talking to the animal. "Hello, Ouoji," she said. "Still barred from the teleport, I see."

Ouoji squeezed her eyes as though accepting the rule which Siggerson had laid down after she managed to switch on the equipment and nearly sent herself into oblivion. But without warning she leapt past Beaulieu and into the room, where she inspected a plainly startled Arnaht with much sniffing and little burrs of inquiry.

"What is this thing?" demanded Arnaht, drawing away.

"Ouoji!" said Siggerson. "Out of here now! You know the rules."

Ouoji lashed her long tail and ignored Siggerson while she circled Arnaht.

Siggerson turned on Beaulieu. "Why did you let her in here? You know what ouoji hair does to the—"

"I didn't!" Beaulieu snapped. "You set up the rule. You enforce it. Arnaht, will you come with me, please?"

The Salukan stepped gingerly past Ouoji and came out into the corridor. A klaxon went off. Arnaht threw himself against a wall, and Siggerson came bolting from the teleport bay.

"What is it?" asked Beaulieu, although she didn't need telling. Obviously they'd been spotted. Obviously they'd be blown into small particles in a matter of seconds.

Siggerson ran past her without a glance. She turned to Arnaht and said fiercely, "Go into the galley and strap yourself in one of the chairs. Don't wander about and don't touch any equipment."

Not giving him a chance to answer, she ran after Siggerson.

By the time she reached the flight deck, Siggerson was at his pilot's station with his master control panels flashing all at once.

Beaulieu took her place at the sensors. "We've been scanned," she said.

Working feverishly, Siggerson didn't look up. "Obviously."

"I thought the waver field prevented that."

Siggerson's bony jaw knotted. He didn't reply and Beaulieu figured it was because he'd thought the same thing.

"Now what?" she asked. "If we're no longer invisible, we can't sit here in orbit until—"

"What are you talking about?" he said. "We aren't going to sit here. We—"

She felt a thrum go through the deck beneath her feet. "No! Siggerson, you can't—"

"Power reaching nominal levels," he muttered, ignoring her as he watched his indicators. "Switching to manual control. Prepare for—"

"No!"

She launched herself from her seat and ran to his station, seizing him by one arm and spinning him around. "We can't leave yet."

His eyes, as devoid of emotion as pale chips of ice, gazed into hers. "Don't be stupid. They're dead, or as good as dead. Our orders are to—"

"Our orders are to wait two more hours if the pickup time is missed," she said grimly, aware that he was right. She was being stupid—worse, sentimental. There was nothing logical about denying the facts. But she went on just the same: "We have to give Kelly that chance. If he or any of the others are still trying to make it, then we can't go off and leave them."

"We don't have a choice," said Siggerson. "By now Gamael Central will be tracking us, our position pinpointed, and a squadron on its way."

"Then we can fight."

"For what purpose? We have the man we came for. Kelly

wouldn't appreciate us failing to complete the mission out of a case of mistaken loyalty.''

Beaulieu released him and stepped back, her throat working. Siggerson was right. She knew it. But she also knew she would never stop feeling guilty if they left now without giving Kelly the full amount of time.

''We can leave orbit, evade the Salukans, do whatever we must, but we have to stay in teleport range until the time is up. Siggerson, we owe them that.''

His mouth tightened, but when he glanced angrily at her she knew she'd won. ''We can move our position,'' he said. ''That will strengthen the waver shield and possibly confuse their sensors. Their scanners are using a combination of penetrating microwaves and dense—''

''Never mind,'' said Beaulieu. ''You're the best pilot in the Alliance. If you can't elude a defense squadron, no one can. Just *do* something.''

His gaze dropped from hers. ''Take your position.''

As flimsy as it was, the ruse worked. Dressed in trooper uniforms, Kelly and 41 herded the others across the parade ground where crews of medics and orderlies were systematically cleaning away wounded and dead. A detachment of troopers marched past them in strict formation and Kelly's nerves stretched into wire, but the troopers spared them no glance.

In the distance sobbing wails could be heard, eerie cries for the dead that sent prickles through Kelly. He glanced across at the tower. Spotlights stabbed down in random search patterns, splashing upon buildings, equipment, and people. Someone scuttled across an open space, trying to duck out of the spotlight. There came a shout and a single shot. The person fell sprawling.

Kelly's grip tightened upon his blaster, and Melaethia flinched visibly. ''Keep walking,'' he said in Saluk.

The trick he had learned long ago in this business was to walk with confidence as though you had every right to be where you were. So far, with Salukans concerned with recouping order, escorting a clutch of prisoners under the supervision of a minlord appeared perfectly normal. No one questioned them.

On the far side of the barracks, however, it got harder. They had no business taking prisoners here, and if they lingered too long among the parked shuttles and airsleds they were bound to be noticed.

Melaethia, Caesar, and Phila melted into the shadows, and Kelly and 41 walked on alone to find what they needed. They had to appear unhurried, yet urgency thudded inside Kelly with every crunching step upon the gravel. The city perimeters were closed now; airspace would be under detection watch. Even if they got out, they had nowhere to hide in the desert, with its sensor grid that would register their landing.

Be there for us, Siggerson, he prayed.

He stopped in front of an airsled, peering at it through the gloomy backwash from the light over the sentry's post.

41 grunted. "Not big enough."

Beside the airsled was a needle-thin craft able to seat only one. It had heavy laser cannons bolted to its undercarriage and a sleekness that made Kelly ache to try it out.

He pressed his palm to the polished hull. "A beauty, 41."

41 tapped his sleeve and pointed. At first Kelly couldn't see it.

"That shuttle?"

"No," said 41, compressing his words even more than usual. "Too big. Too slow. There."

It was a long airsled with double seats. Enough room to hold them all. Remembering his airsled ride on Chealda with 41, Kelly grinned.

"Has it got a crest painted on the side?"

41 chuckled softly. "I wish it had the Pharaon's seal, but I see nothing. It will do. Break the lock and let us—"

Hearing something, Kelly grabbed his arm in warning. 41 winced, and Kelly quickly loosened his grip.

"I hear," breathed 41. "One man approaching. The sentry?"

Kelly nodded, tensing himself. "Get the others loaded," he said. "I'll deal with him."

41 hesitated uncharacteristically. "Kelly—"

"Go!"

41 disappeared into the shadows, and Kelly moved as quietly as the gravel would permit toward the direction of the sentry. It would have to be a dirty ambush. He was in no shape for a fight. His bandage still held, but the wound felt as though it could open again at the least exertion. Anything more strenuous than a careful walk left him dizzy and weak. The painkiller had worn off long ago.

"I see you clearly," said the sentry from the darkness.

Kelly paused and glanced around. A shuttle loomed behind him; he had the sleek little one-seater on his right. Unease prickled through him. He didn't like his opponent being able to see better than he did. He took another step forward.

"Don't move!"

Stall for time, Kelly told himself. Give the others a chance.

The blaster grip, designed for nonhuman hands, slipped against his sweaty palm. He wanted to squeeze off a couple of shots, but he didn't want to alert the entire garrison. Or maybe the sentry had already sounded a silent alarm and was stalling for reinforcements.

Kelly steadied himself, knowing he couldn't worry about that now. His people were getting out of here and that was all he cared about.

"There is no need to be so quiet," said his opponent, coming still closer. Kelly could see him now, a shadow moving slowly, steadily, confidently. Kelly frowned.

A sentry would be running, trying to make an arrest and shouting for attention. Who was this?

"Vaudan," he said aloud.

The other stopped abruptly. "A clever guess. Or perhaps Earthers see better in the dark than I thought."

"I'm surprised you're not calling yourself Pharaon now."

The vaudan laughed. "Tomorrow will be soon enough for that. I did not expect you to escape. That shows admirable cunning and a determination to survive. I have heard this said of your species. Now I see for myself that it is true."

"Cut the compliments," said Kelly brusquely. "This isn't a tea social."

"As you say." The vaudan's voice turned cold. "Where are the others?"

"Who?"

"Don't be a fool. Your men. Where have you left them?"

"Still in the interrogation area," said Kelly quickly. "I'm scouting for an escape route."

"You lie. Your men are here with you, trying to steal a shuttle. That's futile. The force wall goes over the top of Byiul."

Kelly's hopes sank, but he pushed himself past emotion. He'd set a course of action; he would carry it through.

The vaudan came closer, holding his weapon on Kelly. "You will call your men out of hiding now."

Kelly's own blaster was aimed right back at the vaudan. If they both fired, they would both die.

A whistling crackle came over his comm. "Boss?" said Caesar's voice. "We're ready and waiting."

Kelly didn't hesitate. Lifting his wristband to his mouth, he said, "Lift off now. That's an order!"

"*Achei!*" yelled the vaudan in a fury. The rest of his sentence, however, was drowned out by the sound of the airsled rising straight up.

Kelly watched it go, knowing they didn't have a chance to break through the barrier unless he gave it to them.

The vaudan fired at him, but Kelly was already diving to the ground. He rolled frantically to his right, and the blaster barely missed him. Scrambling beneath the one-seater, Kelly came up on the other side, clutching his stomach with one hand and the blaster with his other. He fired back, and the vaudan fell with a scream.

Kelly shot the electronic hatch lock, and the hatch sprang open. The interior light came on automatically. He scrambled in, his legs and feet tangling around a central pylon of controls which he had to straddle. It was a tight enough fit for him; he wondered how the taller Salukans managed to fold themselves into one of these.

Closing the hatch, he activated the engines, and the slim craft fairly vibrated as power came up. He watched the line indicators flash to life, hoping he was reading the controls correctly. Swiftly he located steering, throttle, armament.

Someone pounded on the hull, reaching for the hatch. Startled, Kelly hit the controls harder than he intended and the craft clawed its way into the air with a scream of power that mashed him into his seat and left his stomach somewhere behind.

A spotlight from the tower blinded him despite the compensating polarization from the windscreen. He tried to level off, found the steering four times more sensitive than he expected, overcompensated, and nearly went into an uncontrolled roll. Managing to straighten, he saw the side of the tower coming up too fast. With a gasp he tilted and scraped past.

Squawking static came over the comm. Kelly did not try to tune in the frequency. He activated his scanner and located the airsled flying 71.7 meters ahead of him, direction bearing one mark five, distance closing.

Kelly settled himself in. All he had to do was overtake them and get ahead. Then his plan had better work or they'd bounce off that force wall and end up as two long smears on the streets of Byiul.

A blast rocked the one-seater, nearly spinning it out of control as Kelly inadvertently overcompensated again. This baby needed a feather touch, and who was firing at him?

Another blast bumped him from underneath. By then Kelly had located the artillery on the tower. He increased power and charged his own two laser cannons. The deck beneath him shuddered as the firing muzzles ran out and locked into active-use position.

Tapping up the speed, he lifted the nose and curved straight up and over, falling out of the roll just in time to keep his craft together. That fancy maneuver brought him facing the tower, level with the top. He screamed past the artillery guns trying to reset their range in time to get him point-blank. Kelly hit both firing buttons.

The craft recoiled as the cannons blazed away. His target lock-on registered a direct hit before a huge ball of flame belched out of the artillery control slot and engulfed the sky.

The explosion rocked Kelly, and he sent his craft rolling into a short dive, leveling out quickly in order to gain on the airsled again.

He dared take a hand off the controls just long enough to wipe the sweat from his face. The interior of the one-seater was roasting. There must be little insulation in the bulkhead separating him from the power drive. His shoulders brushed the sides of the craft and he felt jammed up and unable to move freely.

He wanted to think they were getting out, but he kept his attention locked on his scanner. It wasn't over yet.

A whistle came over his wristband comm. "Boss? Is that you on our tail?"

Kelly grinned. "That's right, Caesar. Tell 41 to slow down a notch. I've got to come ahead of you."

There was a short pause before Caesar came back: "Uh, boss. 41's taking a little nap right now, so Phila is doing the driving. We're slowing now as per orders. Any other instructions? We're getting a warning light. Is that the perimeter wall?"

Kelly's mouth dried out. "Yes," he said. He checked his scanner; no one coming after them yet. Obviously the Salukans were waiting for the wall to put an end to this escape ride.

Kelly set his jaw and tapped the throttle. He surged ahead of the airsled, flicking his cannon charges to full power. They had one slim, stupid chance. He had to make it work. A blue warning light began to flash in front of him. He felt his speed kick off just for a split second. Fear clutched him. What if this craft was designed to switch to autopilot to avoid collision?

There was only one way to find out. Sweating harder, he kept going.

"Uh, boss," said Caesar's voice. "Definitely approaching a force wall. We can't go over the top, and we can't go through. Instructions, please."

Kelly tried to swallow, but his throat wasn't working too well. "Listen close," he said. "I'm going to make a hole, and you've got to go through it. That calls for tricky flying, but it's our only chance. Do you copy?"

Silence from the airsled. Kelly gritted his teeth. "Do you copy?"

"Yes," said Caesar's voice, sounding small and tight. "We copy. Phila says she'll bull's-eye it. How about you?"

Kelly didn't know yet. He hoped he could follow before the weakening effect his cannon fire would have on the force wall mended itself. The risks were astronomical. He preferred not to think about them.

"Don't worry about me," he sent back. "Stand by. Firing now."

He cut speed to allow the airsled to pull closer. Setting aim on maximum spread, he fired on the force wall, and for a few seconds it became visible to the naked eye as raw energy pulses of white and blue crackled through its thickness and radiated outward.

His theory was that the force wall, which was a network of tightly oscillating energy waves, would redirect its power spread to maximize at the spot where Kelly was firing, thus weakening itself in a nearby section.

He slowed his speed, flipping over to hover mode barely in time to save his craft from stalling. Below he could see housetops with small figures standing on them.

"Enjoy the fireworks, folks," he said grimly, and kept continuous fire going. At this rate he'd exhaust his charge in a brief matter of minutes, but that was all he needed.

The airsled sailed past him, moving at a reduced but steady speed. He hoped Phila had enough piloting skill to judge sufficient speed to breach the weakened force wall. Too much speed could be as bad as not enough.

A blip on his scanner caught the corner of his eye. He blinked and took a second look with a sinking heart. Outside the perimeter, hovering above the desert, was a wing of defense craft just waiting on the slim chance that they made it through. The unarmed airsled would be an easy target for them.

Kelly adjusted his comm frequency. "Kelly to *Valiant*. Come in, please. This is an emergency. Are you there?"

He had no time to listen for a reply, however. The airsled hit the force wall and a tremendous shriek of conflicting energy and turbulence filled the air, penetrating even through the hull of Kelly's one-seater. He winced and his eardrums felt as though they had been shredded.

But the airsled was going through. He saw it waver, the illusion of the ripple effect making it look cut in half. But despite rivulets of blue and white energy running over it, the airsled made it. It didn't immediately crash, which meant its electrical circuits weren't shorted out either.

Judging that the force wall would strengthen itself where the airsled passed through, Kelly changed from hover mode to flight and shot forward. He had to wait until the last possible moment to suspend firing. The blue warning light flashed frantically in front of his eyes.

He felt the shock of impact as the slim nose of his craft pierced the wall. He almost didn't suspend firing quickly enough and the laser backwash nearly caught him. Snapping, sizzling, crackling noises spat around him. His steering controls heated so fast it was all he could do to keep his hands on them. He felt the craft go partway through, then lurch back.

Panicking, Kelly tapped the throttle, and the one-seater strained through with a mighty tearing and ripping and frying of circuits. Figuring he was due for electrocution, Kelly took his hands off the controls, then realized that was stupid since the rest of his body was in contact. He felt as though he was being crushed. He couldn't catch his breath. He couldn't see. The hideous shriek of tortured energy and metal deafened him.

He felt rather than heard the sharp crumple in his tail. The craft's nose tilted at a crazy angle. He fought to lift, but it was too late. He was through the force wall, but he was going down and there was nothing he could do to stop it.

Someone was calling him frantically on the comm. Kelly ignored that. He saw the ground rushing at him, unbelievably fast; he heard the plummeting whine that ended with only one final kind of sound. For a split second his mind went white and smooth with terror, and then he was incredibly, surprisingly calm. He could do nothing more. Death, when it came in a few seconds, would be merciful and instant, like a sudden blacking out. There would be no pain.

He did not often second-guess himself, but in his last moment he thought about his life and the kind of man he was. He hoped his epitaph would say nothing flowery and untrue. He thought of his family—his parents, Drew, Kevalyn, and little J.J., who was not so little anymore. She would be graduating soon from the Academy. He'd wanted to be there for that. He thought of the gorgeous, gray-eyed biochemist he'd met on Station 4 and the plans they'd made for his next leave. So much unfinished. So much undone . . .

The impact filled his world, and he had only the briefest cognizance of his legs shattering before everything went black and cold and final.

14

And wonder stirred the land while the gods walked. Gam herself received them willingly, taught them, and nourished them. Then she sent them forth again, upon the sea, upon the wind, and upon the sky, to be greater than she, to be her sons and daughters in all places.

—from the Sacred Scrolls, IX

Sensation first, a hazy swirl of grayness with neither hearing nor sight nor feel, a pleasant limbo of nothing. Later came thought, a wondering of *Can this be death*? despite a vague suspicion that it was not.

Kelly's eyes dragged open, feeling as though they were weighted down with trinium bricks. He saw a collage of blurred shapes and colors. The light was so bright it hurt him. Letting his eyes fall shut, he escaped back into dark safety.

A thousand years later he heard soft music—no singing, just gentle string instrumentals in some antique Earth pattern of melody. He liked it and he opened his eyes, finding them much less heavy this time.

Thoughts drifted like cloudpuffs inside his skull.

He lay in a bed. No. He floated somehow from the waist down. Frowning, Kelly made an effort to pull his observations together.

His back was supported by a gentle incline, but his legs were floating in some kind of sloppy green gel. He felt no discomfort beyond thirst. A general haze of well-being told him he was probably drugged to the gills.

So where was he? How had he gotten here?

Slowly, dimly, he remembered the escape attempt. Faces and pieces of action came floating back in a confused pattern. He'd been flying, trying to get away.

The crash.

With sudden clarity it came back to him. He'd crashed after going through the force wall. Somehow, unbelievably he'd survived.

How? He should have been pulp.

Maybe he was. Maybe what he thought he saw was the effect of a strong hallucinogen to make him think he was still whole. He might be nothing more than a few bits of brain tissue still clumped together enough to hold consciousness, still enough to be pried at by the Salukan interrogators.

"No!" he screamed, breaking out in a sudden sweat. He gripped the sides of his bed. "No!"

The music stopped. Someone came running. Cool, strong hands gripped him, soothed him, pressed him back. After a moment his heart stopped beating so wildly. He drew a breath, then another as his adrenaline shook down. Shakily he wiped his face and dared look at his world again.

Beaulieu's dusky, angular face gazed down at him. Her ears were still pointed but she had her grizzled, short-cropped hair back and her eyelid tucks were gone. She wore the black and silver uniform of the Space Hawks with the taloned emblem on her left shoulder.

"Take it easy," she said. "Some of the stuff in your bloodstream is pretty potent."

Her slim dark hand, both nimble-fingered and strong, rested easily upon his wrist. Kelly gripped it.

"Beaulieu?" His voiced sounded pathetic. The two syllables exhausted him. His head tipped back. "Real? Or . . ." He trailed off.

She smiled and for once her eyes were gentle and soft with warmth. "I'm real, Commander. Siggerson waited almost too late to teleport you out of that thing. 41 says he should have his legs broken to know how it feels, but the rest of us are just glad that you're here.''

Kelly smiled back, drinking in her words, absorbing them one by one.

He must have dozed off, for when he awakened again the lights were brighter above him and the music had changed. Beaulieu appeared at his side with a soft squeeze-globe of liquid. She held it to his lips, and he sipped gratefully.

The interlude had helped. His mind felt much clearer. ''I made it,'' he said slowly. ''I thought . . .''

Her hand gripped his firmly. ''You're alive and you're on the *Valiant* heading home. Your stomach wound is nearly healed and we've got your legs packed in regenerative gel that's loaded with all kinds of local anesthesia and nutrients to keep the torn ligaments, blood vessels, and so on as supported as possible until real surgery can be performed. You'll be as good as new in a few months.''

He began, at last, to believe it might all be true. ''The others,'' he said.

''Everyone's fine.'' She placed her hand on his chest. ''Don't start worrying about anyone. You can have visitors, one at a time, for one minute each. Then it's plenty of rest for you.''

He nodded meekly and she stepped back with a gesture at someone.

Siggerson came in first, bony, balding, oblivious to most things besides piloting the ship. Ouoji lay draped across his shoulders, looking huge and sleek. She squeezed her blue eyes at Kelly and Kelly smiled back.

He shook Siggerson's hand. ''I hear I have you to thank for saving my life.''

Siggerson turned bright red. ''Nonsense,'' he said brusquely. ''Beaulieu did everything but sabotage the ship in order to get me to stick past the pickup time. We got shot up a bit, but no serious damage. I'd like, however, on this trip back, to try a couple of modifications on the engine transfer couplings that I've been—''

''Siggerson,'' said Beaulieu sternly. ''Your time is up.''

Ouoji bounded off his shoulder and took up a new position on Beaulieu's examining table.

''No, you can't stay,'' said Beaulieu. ''Siggerson, get this beast out of my sick bay.''

''Let her stay,'' said Kelly.

Lifting his head weakly, he managed a wink at Ouoji. She lashed her bushy tail back and forth in complete accord. Beaulieu looked from one of them to the other and gave in with a roll of her eyes.

Siggerson shuffled obediently out and Caesar bounded in with his hair as red and unruly as ever. His skin, however, remained blue.

''Hey, boss, have you got it made, or what?'' he said with such exuberance Kelly felt tired. ''You might want to consult another doctor. This one can't get the dye neutralized out of my skin. Who knows what she'll do with fractures?''

''I fixed yours, didn't I?'' snapped Beaulieu. ''Out.''

Caesar grinned and gripped Kelly's hand very hard. ''Don't scare us like that anymore, boss. Our nerves can't stand it.''

''I'll . . . try,'' said Kelly.

Phila was still limping from her leg wound. ''We match,'' she said ''I get green goop smeared on me once a day.''

Arnaht and Melaethia—rounder and more contoured than Kelly had last seen her—came in together.

''Thank you,'' said Arnaht with simple dignity. ''We owe our lives and our freedom to you. Thank you for restoring my daughter safely to me. I am sorry my son caused so much trouble.''

Salukans did not shake hands. Kelly inclined as best he could. ''It was an honor to assist you, sir. I hope you will find life comfortable on Minza when you settle there.''

''No,'' said Melaethia, speaking heavily accented Glish. ''We have changed our minds. We choose instead to live among you Earthers. You are not so strange to us now and the children will prosper among you.''

Kelly blinked. ''Children?''

''Melaethia,'' said Beaulieu proudly, ''is going to have triplets and she intends to name them after all of us.''

''I . . . see,'' said Kelly. ''Uh, congratulations.''

Something in that drink Beaulieu gave him must have had a sedative in it. He felt suddenly groggy. His eyes began to slip shut, but he fought off the effect, not wanting to miss 41.

"Enough visits," said Beaulieu. "We've tired you out with too much all at once."

"No," he said thickly. "41."

"I am here," said 41's voice.

With effort Kelly dragged his eyes open and saw 41's white, rather pointed teeth bared in the fierce grimace he used for a smile. Right now 41 was actually beaming. His yellow eyes met Kelly's blue ones and in that moment they needed no words.

"I will always be here," said 41. He looked at Beaulieu. "Do not argue. I will stay while he sleeps."

Seating himself at Kelly's bedside, he reached out for Ouoji, who chittered happily and came bounding into his lap. She did not like to be petted, but she did stretch her neck far enough for Kelly to briefly touch her head. Then she snuggled up against 41 as though to say she meant to stay.

"Now look, you two," began Beaulieu, but 41 and Ouoji just stared at her and did not budge. She threw up her hands. "Oh, all right. But be quiet. He needs his rest."

"We'll guard his rest," said 41 firmly, and Beaulieu dimmed the lights.

When she was gone and Kelly was drifting off into a comfortable fog, 41 touched his face gently.

"Sleep, Kelly," he murmured. "Sleep with no bad dreams."

And Kelly slept.